NOBODY CAN PRONOUNCE MY NAME

Robert McGee

Praise for *Nobody Can Pronounce My Name*

"Robert McGee writes laugh-out-loud short stories that always seem to go in exactly the direction you didn't expect and drop you off on an entirely wrong corner that is a little bit darker but much more pleasant than the one you had planned to visit."

—Dylan Brody, award-winning humorist, author, and playwright

"Nobody Can Pronounce My Name is a fun and eclectic mix of short stories. McGee's adventures and the worlds he builds will have you rolling on the floor. I highly recommend!"

—Ginny Hogan, author of *Toxic Femininity in the Workplace*

"Robert tells the story of an American moving to Germany with humor, class, and words like 'Zweihundertsechsundzwanzig.' I'm pretty sure pronouncing that three times will summon demons, but I can't be sure. I am sure that teaching English is a tough gig under normal circumstances and Robert's account of doing it in Germany with middle-aged businessmen who would rather be at the pub had me rolling scene after scene. Great book, great read!"

—Shannon Carpenter, American Humorist

"As a fellow American living in Germany, I can attest that Rob is not making any of this up. He eloquently and humorously captures the struggle of making a home and a family abroad while maintaining one's own sense of self and cultural identity—no easy task. I saw myself in it, although I must admit I do answer the phone the German way: KNOTT!"

—Jenn Knott, Comedy and parenting writer, *Slackjaw, The Belladonna, Hallo Eltern*

"It takes an observant writer to create funny and perceptive stories out of the process of adapting to a new life in a new country. Robert McGee's pieces are an interesting blend of cultural insight and humor, and make for an enjoyable book."

—James Folta, writer and editor

for Eva

Contents

Leave it to June

My first teaching job was as a philosophy and logic instructor at the University of Missouri-Columbia, the research campus of the University of Missouri system. It was an above average Midwest school in a state no sane person would want to live in.

When I moved to Germany to start a family with Sandra, I landed a job as an English lecturer in the language center at the University of Saarland, a moderately sized university in Saarbrücken, the capital city of a German state no sane person would want to live in.

It was a lateral move career-wise.

A few weeks after the interview, I returned to turn in a photo for my staff ID and to pick up the key to my room. The department's secretary informed me that my class would meet in the Sprachlabor on the third floor. *Cool*, I thought, *a language laboratory*. I wasn't exactly sure what a language laboratory was though —what experiments did people preform on students trying to learn English? Could I shock them if they mispronounced too many words?

After signing for the key, I headed up to the third floor to check out the room. At first glance, it looked to be relatively well-equipped: all of the desks had integrated computers, a digital projector was mounted on the ceiling, and there were speakers in the corners — movie day wouldn't be a problem and I briefly wondered if I could come up with a pedagogical reason to watch *Faster Pussycat! Kill! Kill!* with my class.

I turned on the computer at my desk, and, after some grinding sounds, was greeted by a Windows 95 logo. Shocked, I immediately hit the power button and the computer shut off with a satisfying clunk. Ten years isn't a long time to go without cauliflower, but it's an unforgivably long time for a university to go without updating its computers. Missouri didn't seem so primitive anymore.

I didn't find any shock collars in the room, so I locked up and went out to explore. The campus wasn't exactly dead, but it did lack the pulse of what I had come to expect from American campuses. In the States, the students essentially lived on campus and they did their best to make it feel like home. When I walked around Missouri's campus, I would see students having picnics on the lawns, reading groups under trees, or drinks in the parking lot. Once, I had even seen students practicing for their anatomy class in the bushes, but the only group of people I saw on Saarland's campus was the group waiting for a bus.

Slightly disheartened, I decided to check out the coffee shop, remembering that when I was a university student, the local coffee shop was a second home—mostly because I was too young to live at the bar.

The café was big enough for three tables. It had seven. After squeezing past two of the tables and politely kicking someone's backpack out of the way to get to the counter, I ordered in my best German.

The barista looked like those of my youth—at least those I cared to remember anyway—slightly punk, painfully thin, and with an expression that dared you to mispronounce 'venti.' I liked her immediately. She heard my accent and answered in English, but I figured that since I was getting paid to speak English now, I shouldn't just give away English practice for free, so I continued the conversation in German. I didn't like her well enough to work for free, and she didn't seem to mind. Much.

After the coffee, I headed towards the bus stop—peaking into bushes along the way—and went home.

A few days later, an email arrived from my new boss detailing some of the finer points of the job. A lot of it had been covered in the interview, but two details stuck out. The first was that my classes would be at eight o'clock in the morning, which would be a minor annoyance since I had a tendency to stay up late and drink too much. But the second detail made me nervous: I wouldn't be paid until after the semester was over. I had assumed I would be paid monthly, as I had been in Missouri, but it was now clear that I wouldn't be seeing any money for quite some time. Sandra could cover the rent for a little while, but that was only part of the problem. Insurance was the real problem.

Germany requires everyone to have health insurance, which is nice, but since I was an American on a freelance contract, the powers that be assumed I was wealthy enough to pay for the much more expensive private insurance, which was not nice. While it angered me that Germany wanted Americans to teach English and also wanted those Americans to be poor, there was nothing I could do about it. I had to find another job. And Soon.

In the back of my head, a nervous voice told me that this situation was financially untenable without Sanra's help, but I told him to be quiet.

I logged out of my email and searched for language schools in the Saarbrücken area. There weren't many, but, as far as I could tell, there also weren't too many English speakers in the area either, so I figured my chances were good.

One private school, Brandt Languages, looked promising, but their requirements were a bit confusing. They wanted applicants to have a university degree, which made sense, but they also wanted applicants to submit a photo with the application, which made no sense. I could understand wanting to have an attractive secretary, but wanting attractive teachers was just offensive. Not that I was ugly, of course. It was the principle of the matter.

I decided to apply anyway, and then discovered that the online application submission form was broken. Luckily for me, however, their incompetent website designer was, well, incompetent, so with a little digging through the site's code, I was able to figure out the email address of the school. I typed up a quick cover letter, attached my CV, did not attach a photo, and raised my glass to toast my father for teaching me how to use computers before most people had computers in their houses.

There weren't any other schools within walking distance of my apartment, so I looked for other jobs in the vicinity that needed native English speakers. There were only two that I could find, and since I didn't have the right genitals to work at the brothel that serviced the US Army base, I sent my CV to a small academic publishing house. It looked like it would be a cubicle job, but I needed the money. For rent money and health insurance I could be an office whore.

Feeling proud of myself, I finished my drink, wrote Sandra a note telling her not to wait up, and went to the bar.

***

The phone woke me the following morning. With a groan, I grabbed it from the nightstand. "Hello?" I said in my pre-coffee voice.

"Hello. This is Candide Girard from Brandt Languages in Saarbrücken," a female voice answered. "Am I speaking to Robert McGee?"

"Yeah, this is Rob." I rolled over on my back and looked at the ceiling.

"We received your CV and would like to invite you for an interview."

"'Candide' like from the Voltaire novel?" The ceiling needed to be dusted.

"Yes, that's correct. You've read Voltaire?" She seemed a little surprised, which told me a lot about the kind of applicants she was used to.

"Yeah, of course, but I thought 'Candide' was a man's name."

"In French it's a unisex name. I'm French."

"Cool. Umm, sorry for getting distracted. Yes, of course, I'm available for an interview."

"I know it's short notice, but could you come by the school today? I could meet you at twelve if that's convenient for you."

"Yeah, sure. I can do that."

"Very good. I'll see you at twelve o'clock."

After hanging up the phone, I looked over at the clock. I still had a few hours, so I went back to sleep.

When I woke up, it occurred to me that the school was as desperate as I was. Any school that would call me the day after receiving my application would certainly hire me.

I put the coffee on and took a shower.

Not being sure how formal the school was, I decided to wear my beige chinos, a green knit tie and a navy corduroy jacket. After I put on a tweed flat cap, I looked like an English teacher. Or at least some clichéd version of one. I gave my brown brogues a quick brush and headed out. A look at my watch told me I had a half-hour before the interview, and since the school was only fifteen minutes away, I stopped off at the bar for a gin and tonic. It seemed like an appropriate drink for a clichéd English teacher.

I got to the school with a few minutes to spare and introduced myself to the secretary. Being slightly on the heavy side and sitting an a chair that was too low to the ground, gave here a squat, frogish look. She smiled brightly and seemed pleasant enough. Then she gave me an application to fill out, and I didn't like her anymore.

"A lot of this information is already on my CV," I said. "Do I have to fill all of it out?"

"Yes, we need it for our records." She smiled the smile of rule-followers.

"All right." I nodded. "Why can't a CV be used for records?" I thought.

I took the application and sat down at the table in

the reception area and got to work. Things went smoothly enough until the end. They wanted me to write a few paragraphs on my education and work history and explain how this background prepared me for work at the school. For most people this would have been easy enough, but I had always been a terrible speller. I knew lots of words, of course, including quite a few five-dollar words like 'antediluvian,' 'supererogatory,' and the onomato-poeic 'borborygmus,' but I once had to ask Sandra how to spell 'liar.'

Trying my best to pick words I was confident I knew how to spell, and writing the words I wasn't confident about rather sloppily to, hopefully, hide the fact I had a disability which might disqualify me from being an English teacher, I suffered through the essay. The secretary thanked me when I turned it in and called Candide. A few moments later a lithe woman in lose-fitting cotton pants entered the lobby. Candide, I assumed.

"Mr. McGee?" she said.

I nodded and extended my hand.

When she looked down, her glasses slid to the tip of her nose. "Thank you for coming on such short notice."

"No problem. Thanks for inviting me. And, please, call me Rob. What's the old joke? Mr. McGee was my father?"

"I don't know that one, but as you wish. Shall we

go to one of the classrooms to talk? I believe the Twain Room is open."

"The rooms are named after writers?"

"Yes, but I'm sure most our students don't realize that. Most of our students are business people who approach the English language as a job skill rather than as a gateway to English language literature."

Luckily she was walking in front of me and didn't see the look of disgust that I'm sure crossed my face.

The Twain Room was more boardroom than classroom. A conference table filled most of the available space. a whiteboard hung on one wall, and there was a flip chart in a corner on the opposite side of the room. The design, I thought, was probably intended to make the business students more comfortable, but I wasn't sure. What I was sure about was that I would never use that flip chart no matter how at home it would make the business students feel. The sound of markers on paper was high on my list of uncomfortable sounds — a little higher than the sound of drunks singing, a little lower than the sound of people eating.

We sat down at the table and talked about my CV. She seemed interested in the philosophy classes I had taught and the research I had done in Columbia, but I got the impression it was just a personal interest and she had already decided I could have the job if I wanted it.

After a chat about Wittgenstein, she told me the

school required their teachers to complete the school's training sessions. These normally took two weeks, but since I already had teaching experience, I could start teaching my own classes more-or-less immediately and do the training sessions when I could squeeze them in. As long as I finished them within a month, nobody at the head office in Frankfurt would know we had bent the rules. So, Candide was someone who could talk philosophy and didn't care much for the rules. I was starting to like her despite the fact I disliked bosses on principle.

"So, what kinds of classes would I teach here? What are the students like?" I asked after a lull in the conversation.

"We offer group classes and private lessons. The private lessons are almost always for business people but sometimes we get university students who need a little extra help passing their exams. The groups are usually either business groups or from the Arbeitsamt."

I raised an eyebrow. "Arbeitsamt?"

"Sorry. That's the Employment Office. The unemployed in Germany can take various classes or training programs in order to make themselves more marketable. The Arbeitsamt is one of our biggest clients."

"That's pretty cool. How are the students?"

She tilted her head and shrugged her shoulders slightly. "Well, many of them haven't been in a classroom in a long time, and many of them weren't terribly good students when they were last in a class anyway. So, part of what you'll have to do is teach them how to be students."

This statement worried me. I had spent nearly my entire life in classrooms—at one end of the desk or the other, so, to me, being a student was about as natural as breathing. How could I teach someone how to breathe? What wouldn't they know how to do? Write things down? Ask questions when they didn't understand? Take air in through the mouth or nostrils and not through the anus?

"I'm sure I can do that," I lied.

"That's good to hear. These classes are actually one of the reasons we contacted you so quickly. We have three classes starting next week and we don't really have enough teachers to handle the load comfortably. If somebody gets sick, we'll be in trouble."

I had guessed correctly: the school was desperate for teachers. "So, I've got the job?"

"If you want it."

"It sounds interesting," I lied again. "When can I start?" Teaching business people who thought learning English was the intellectual equivalent of learning office productivity software sounded like torture for a guy who knew who Twain was and enjoyed reading him for fun, but the job would pay for the bills and beer.

We went to the secretary to look at the schedule

and make a plan for when I could teach and when I could have a training session. That done, she showed me around the school and explained some of the office policies. I feigned attention until it was time to shake hands and leave.

Just across the street from Brandt stood a pizza place that sold pizza by the slice from a little window, and since I wasn't interested in sitting in any place that didn't serve whiskey, I got a few slices and walked along Bahnhofstrasse towards St. Johanner Markt, the historic downtown area of Saarbrücken. Bahnhofstrasse, literally "Train Station Street," starts, unsurprisingly, at the train station and stretches through the city to St. Johanner Markt, the former red light district but now bar and restaurant district at the heart of the city. I appreciated this historical feature of my new town — the heart of the city is a former whore trying to turn her life around.

While it's true that 'Bahnhofstrasse' is not the most creative name, the lost visitors who stumble upon it do have a fifty-fifty chance of finding the train station, so there is *something* to be said for the name. Go left and find your way home, go right and find your way to a pub. So, you can't really go wrong when you stumble around Saarbrücken as long as you stick close to the main road. I wasn't stumbling yet, so St. Johanner Markt was easy to get to.

There are people in Saarland who insist that the best market area in the state is in Saarlouis and not in Saarbrücken, but these people are wrong. The market in Saarlouis is too open, too big, and entirely too clean. St. Johanner Markt benefits from more authentic-looking cobblestones and its seedier history. A number of the pubs tucked into the white houses that surround the central fountain even retain their former whorehouse names. So, while the people in Saarlouis settled down for an ice cream and looked down at modern pavement or up at a blue sky, I settled down for a beer at a place named after a madam, looked up at a pale stain on the wall, wondered how long it had been there, and didn't want to know what had caused it. It felt like home.

Some time later, when I paid for my drinks, I gave the bartender a tip, but he insisted that it was too much and gave some of it back to me. I thought I was giving him a minimally acceptable tip, but that was just because I hadn't adjusted to German tipping customs. I shrugged my shoulders, pocketed the money he didn't want, finished my whiskey, then left.

It was a nice day and I felt a little guilty for being tipsy before four o'clock, so I decided to take a walk along the river in a vain attempt to sober up a bit before I went home to Sandra. She had told me that the rule in Germany was 'kein Beir vor vier,' which roughly translates to, "don't drink before four o'clock." Good advice that I, and many of the other people in Saarbrücken, consistently ignored.

The park along the river, which the locals called

'Staden,' was really quite nice. Its design was, I was told, inspired by the parks in France, particularly those in Paris. Since Saarland shares a border and intertwined history with France, there's a considerable amount of French influence in the area. The fact that there was a noisy highway which ran directly along the length of the park on the opposite side of the river attested to this theory. On my side of the river, however, there was a paved walking path which snaked through well-manicured lawns, and unlike the well-maintained lawns in Paris, the people here were allowed to walk on the grass. So, overall, Saarbrücken had the edge over the Parisian parks in terms of overall utility.

When I got home, the house was empty. I saw that the light on the answering machine was blinking and considered ignoring it but then thought that it was probably just Sandra asking me to go shopping for dinner, so I listened. And I was right. Almost. Sandra said she was going out with her friends from work to watch some soccer game so I was on my own for dinner. The second message was from the academic publishing house that I had applied to. They wanted me to call back to schedule an interview.

I listened to the messages again so I could write down the number of the publishing house and the name of the contact person, but I couldn't quite make out what the name was. Advaith? Advay? I tried to listen a third time but accidentally hit the erase button. I wondered if he would care if I just called him Ad. In any case, the bigger challenge would be not to slur together the words I knew how to pronounce, but since I already had two jobs, there wasn't much pressure.

With minimal difficulty, I got through to Ad and scheduled an interview.

The grocery stores, along with most other businesses, were required by law to close at eight o'clock, but that was still a few hours away, so I headed back out thinking I would wander a bit before settling down for the evening. As I walked around a corner, a stiff wind reminded me that I should get a haircut. There was no shortage of hairdressers in Saarbrücken so I didn't have to walk far before I found one. They wanted thirty euros for a cut and a wash, and since I was pretty sure that didn't come with complimentary full body massage, I kept walking until I found another place.

The price at the next place was also a bit high, but the coiffeuse's blouse was cut a bit low, so I splurged. I didn't even ask for a massage.

On my way home, I stopped in a corner market and picked up a frozen pizza, a six-pack of beer, a bottle of gin, and a lime. I wasn't sure when Sandra would be home, so after I got my pizza in the oven and the lime slice in my glass of gin, I sat down to watch Paul Verhoeven's masterpiece, *Robocop*, a secretly brilliant satire of my home country wrapped up in the kind of mindless violence that paired well with pizza.

After the film, Sandra still wasn't home, so I queued up a few episodes of *Leave It to Beaver* and stretched out on the sofa. I liked the show but had always wished they had done an episode that followed June around for the day instead of Beaver. What did she do in that house all day after serving the boys breakfast and ushering them off to school? Her life seemed empty, maybe oppressively so.

Sandra woke me with a kiss and we relocated to the bedroom.

***

After some coffee the next morning, I got out the sewing machine Sandra had bought me. I had picked up a few shirts for work a few days previously, and they still needed to be tailored because it was nearly impossible to find shirts that fit off the rack. When they fit in the chest and across the waist, the arms were way too short. According to shirt manufacturers, tall men are a sub-species of Tyrannosaurs. When I did manage to find a shirt with the proper wingspan, I'd have to grow a gigantic belly and man-tits to fill out the rest. This, of course, wasn't possible before classes began, so I slimmed those shirts down on my machine.

The slimming process would have been easier with a sewing mannequin, but I wasn't quite ready to have one of those in my apartment—I was sure it would scare the hell out of me at some point when I stumbled in after a night at the bar. So, I used myself in front of a mirror. I pinched the shirt together with clothespins to test the size, then together with some measuring tape, I followed the clothespins' suggestions to draw my lines with a fabric pencil. Lines in place, I would pin up the shirt and then try it on again in front of the mirror, this time trying hard not to stab myself with the pins. If everything looked right, I would sit down at the machine to sew it up, check the fit, and cut out the extra material.

Partway through my second shirt, the phone rang. It was Candide from the Brandt School. One of the teachers had just called in sick, and they needed me to fill in the next day.

"I know it's short notice," she said, "and you haven't had any training yet, so don't feel too bad when things go wrong."

"When things go wrong? Thanks for the pep-talk. You should write motivational speeches."

She giggled. "It's OK to be new. That's all I meant."

"Or maybe posters for office bathrooms. When things go wrong, just remember that it's OK to be new."

"Maybe I'll do that if the school goes out of business."

"Good plan. So, is there anything else I should know?"

"No, not really. He's a business student who wants to work on some basic email skills. Polite language, asking for appointments, and so on. We have an email book you can use for ideas. I can show it to you when you come in tomorrow."

"OK. I'll see you tomorrow."

I went back to my sewing. The second shirt turned out better than I had hoped, so I threw on some chinos and went to show Sandra. She had her nose buried in a book, and from the shape it was clearly one of her young adult fantasy books rather than a philosophy book. Apparently, she needed a break from work reading.

"Hey, what to you think?" I ran my fingers through my new haircut and then did my best runway model impression.

She glanced up. "Looks good." And then looked by to her book. "It makes you look like you've lost weight."

"Why go to the gym when you can just cut up your clothes? Not that I need to go to the gym, of course."

"No, you don't need to yet, but the German lifestyle is being kind to you." Apparently, she hadn't noticed the haircut. I wasn't surprised. It normally took her a few days.

"The German lifestyle is just getting me up to normal. When you met me, I was a grad student who didn't have time to eat."

"Yeah, you were skinny back then." She turned a

page.

I went back to the kitchen to pack up my sewing equipment. "Skinny," I muttered under my breath.

My alarm didn't go off the next morning, or it did go off and I didn't hear it, but either way I was nearly late to my first day at work. I apologized to Candide for not showing up sooner to prepare. She didn't seem worried and showed me where the books were. I grabbed the one I needed and headed to the Faulkner Room.

When I entered, my student stood up to shake hands. His subtlety-pinstriped navy suit had obviously been tailored—the waist had been suppressed and the sleeves were just long enough to allow a bit less than an inch of linen to peak out. Unfortunately, he was wearing black shoes with that navy suit, which showed a certain lack of experience with men's fashion. To make matters worse, his socks matched his shoes, which showed that at least part of his trouble with fashion was that he was German. He probably wore those socks with sandals when he went out on the weekend.

"Hi, how are you?" I asked.

"Oh, not so good."

Germans had a hard time answering the simple 'how are you?' For some strange reason they thought it was a genuine question rather than what it really was: a longer way to say hello.

"I'm sorry to hear that," I replied. I wasn't sure

what I was supposed to say. I wasn't prepared to hear someone's life story. I had just wanted to say hi.

He sat back down. "My chef is making me stressed." But the life story would continue, apparently.

"Your chef?" The suit suggested the guy was pretty well off, but I hadn't expected he was well off enough to have a chef

"Yes. He gives me too much work and then gets angry when I fall behind."

"Your chef gives you work to do? That's strange." I shot him a confused look.

"Not really. That's normal."

"Well, if you don't like him, why don't you fire him?" I asked.

"I can't fire my chef." He seemed shocked I would suggest something so clearly insane.

"Why not? He works for you, doesn't he?"

"No, he owns the company. I work for him." This conversation was devolving into the surreal. I thought we should just skip the email lesson and move straight to Lewis Carroll.

"Now, I'm confused. Your chef owns the company that you work for and he cooks your food?"

"My chef doesn't cook my food." Now, I could tell he thought I really was insane.

"OK, so something is not right here. I think we are having a vocabulary problem. Do you have a dictionary?"

"Yes."

"Is 'chef' a German word?"

"Yes. And English, too, or?"

The 'or' stuck onto the end of his sentence made me think there would be more to listen to, but nothing followed other than an awkward pause caused by me not knowing 'or' was the German way of tuning statements into questions. "Yes," I said, "'chef' is an English word, but it's not the right word here. Look it up and read me what it says."

"OK." He thumbed through his pocket dictionary. "Oh. It says that 'chef' is 'boss' or 'manager.'"

"OK. Now your story makes sense. A chef is a person who cooks food in a restaurant. You've got a boss problem, not a chef problem."

I felt a bit guilty that my German wasn't good enough to spot that simple false friend, but I had always hated business and hadn't yet bothered to learn too many business words in German. My language skills were better suited for the bar, the restaurant, or the gynecologist's office.

I made a mental note to put together some lecture notes on business English.

An hour later, I had successfully completed my first class as an English teacher in a foreign country and was pretty sure the student would be happy to go back to his previous English teacher. But I didn't feel too bad about the missteps. It was OK to be new.

After class, Candide told me they had gotten

enough students to fill an Arbeitsamt class. It would start next week, and I would teach them three times a week from eight to three o'clock with a forty-five minute lunch break in the middle. And potentially, I might have to pick up other days if one of the other teachers got sick, or bored. We sat down and made a schedule. On the days I didn't teach, I would do the training sessions. So, for the next few weeks at least, I would be at the school every day. I wasn't looking forward to that. No matter how cool a job is, it's still a job. No sane person had ever lain on his deathbed and said, 'You know, I really wish I had spent more time at the office.'

When I got home, I called the publishing house and told them that I had found another job and would not be coming in for an interview. Academic books or not, it was still a job in a cubicle.

***

Over the next few weeks, I did very little except teach Arbeitsamt classes, which I must admit were rather brilliant from a political point of view. The people in them didn't count as being unemployed, so there was always extra money for these programs during election years because the classes pushed the unemployment numbers down. Plus, the classes were popular with voters, and certainly did help some people find jobs since part of what we taught was how to write a good resume and how to answer interview questions. It didn't take me long to realize the only downside was that I hated teaching them.

Sometimes I got lucky and had a group of interesting and interested students who were happy to get a free English course and took full advantage of the opportunity, but these were rare. More often than not, the groups were full of people who took the class because they got better unemployment benefits if they made an effort to become more employable, even though they weren't actually interested in becoming more employable and didn't actually make any effort. And every once in a while I'd get stuck in a class with people who hated English, refused to learn it, hated America, and wanted me to know it.

I didn't normally last very long in the really bad classes. If I didn't feel like the stress of teaching an uncooperative class, I'd just tell Candide to move me into another, but sometimes I'd use the classes to practice my classroom-controlling techniques.

Classes tended to have different personalities, so it took a little while to figure out how best to exploit those personalities to create a productive learning environment. My first instinct in the uncooperative adult groups was to treat the students like children—forbidding cell phones, requiring them to raise their hands before speaking, talking to them like they were mental patients, and so on. "Very good vocabulary, Hans-Peter. Can you share with the class other examples of how American culture is *unsophis-*

ticated?" It normally worked, but not always.

If I couldn't control the class with baby talk, I'd have to dig deeper into my bag of tricks. A particularly effective method for controlling overly-talkative students was to stand right beside them before I asked a question. It took a certain kind of bravery to look from my crotch up to my face to get my attention, so they normally just looked down and kept quiet. The crotch also had a silencing effect on those that droned on too long. When it was inches from a student's mouth, that mouth closed. Of course, this only worked in classes where the students were used to me wandering around the room. So I always made it a habit to walk around my classes, just in case I needed to use my crotch as a classroom management tool.

If all else failed, I would do nothing. As soon as someone started talking to a neighbor, I would immediately stop explaining the point, sit on top of my desk, and wait. Teachers are made of patience. Students are not. Eventually, one of the them would get frustrated and start yelling at the others to grow up and pay attention.

When university started, I was happy to see that I didn't need any classroom management techniques. Even though the students were barely out of high school, they acted more adult than the the bulk of the adult students at Brandt. I wasn't exactly sure why this was. It might have had something to do with the fact that at the university I had the power to kick the students out of class, which could result in them spending another semester doing something they didn't really want to do. Or it might have been because to study at a university in Germany the students needed to have graduated from one of the academic high schools, which were considerably more demanding that the other types of high schools in the German secondary education system. Whatever the reason, it was a joy teaching there.

For my first class in the language laboratory, we read a fairy tale about a shoemaker who is visited every night by naked elves who do his work for him. After his wife makes some clothes for the elves, they leave. Part of the class was on writing short stories, so I picked that one because it was an easy-to-understand piece that included the basic element I was lecturing on that day—a plot based on a simple problem and a simple solution. Plus, I liked getting them to talk about what they thought the moral of the story was and what real-life event they thought they story might have been based on, if they thought it had been based on some event at all. Most fairy tales are basic morality tales, but the shoemaker story is ambiguous enough for a discussion. In fact, I was secretly hoping one of the students could explain the story to me. Was it a pro-capitalist story about how we shouldn't reward workers too much lest they lose the motivation to work? Was it a misogynistic story about how wives meddle with, and thereby destroy, shoe businesses? Or maybe it wasn't about shoes at all and was just supposed to tell us to not mess up a good thing by changing the situation. I wasn't sure.

The months stretched on and I fell into a comfortable routine. I would teach in the mornings, nap and watch *Leave It to Beaver* in the afternoon, and then occasionally go back to Brandt to teach an evening class for business people. I quickly discovered that teaching business people Friday evenings was a special sort of torture, so I took that time-slot off my availability. For some strange reason it was hard to get people who had left work early on Friday to concentrate on conditional structures. I didn't blame them. If I had worked in an office all week and had the opportunity to leave early, I would have wanted to go to the bar instead of an English class, too.

Near the end of July, both my university classes and my Arbeitsamt classes were drawing to a close. I could understand why my university students were nervous—their classes actually mattered. What I didn't understand was the nervousness of the Brandt students. We offered no degrees at Brandt, only certificates. And since Brandt wasn't an accredited institution, these certificates were, academically speaking, worth about as much as a coffee shop's customer rewards card.

Even so, in order to make my Brandt students less nervous about the test that didn't matter, we went over everything that would be on that test a day before.

"Rob, I have a question." It was Liza. She was from some Eastern European country, and I was pretty sure she was insane. Not because she clearly hadn't combed through her frizzy blonde hair in month, but because I'd once seen her in the city wearing some kind of cloak, chasing pigeons. But maybe that was just an Eastern European pastime. It's hard to tell sometimes.

"Yes, Liza?"

"Do we need to know about whores for the test?"

"What?" I tried to keep most of the shock out of my voice.

"Whores. You do them. In the day. Whores." She stretched the last 'whores' out an uncomfortably long time.

"No, of course not. You don't need to talk about that. In fact, please don't," I said, but I was thinking *well, I guess you can do them in the day.*

"But whores were in the book. I do whores at home. My husband does whores in the city. In the city, whores are called 'errands.'"

Despite my best efforts, A smile broke through but then it clicked. "Oh, you mean 'chores.' And, yes, there is a vocabulary section on chores."

After class I went home to do some chores. In the day.

***

I stretched the exam for my university students across two meetings because it was too long to do in one. After class on the second day, I packed up all of the exams into my bag, went home, and stacked them on my desk. A to-do pile. I knew as soon as I shifted that pile from to-do to done status, I would be able to relax. And have more than enough money for a weekend I wouldn't remember. So, I got to work.

It was slow going. The volume of work wasn't nearly as bad as what I'd had as a philosophy instructor in Missouri, but it was still a lot. In Missouri, I'd had to grade the final papers and final exams of around seventy students, which amounted to grading close to 1,500 pages of philosophy within two weeks of the semester's end. In Saarbrücken, I had closer to fifty students, and they didn't write philosophy, so it was a welcome change.

After a while, I took a dinner break and then returned to my desk with a bottle of whiskey and a few beers.

When I woke, I discovered that the papers had been graded and stacked neatly on my desk. The shoemaker in that fairy tale was probably just an alcoholic, I thought.

My pounding head demanded attention, so after popping a few ibuprofens and filling the biggest cup in the house with coffee, I laid down on the sofa to watch *Leave It to Beaver.*

Later that evening, Sandra suggested we go out to

dinner to celebrate my first semester as a university lecturer in Germany. I had already gotten back into my pajamas and back into a drink, so I didn't really feel like it, but I eventually caved. I threw on some dark jeans, a t-shirt, and sport coat. Sandra kept her work clothes on—jeans and a white button-up with an odd, frilly collar, and we headed to St. Johanner Markt.

We decided to go to Der Stiefel for some Saarlandish food. I had suggested Disconto Schenke, which was my favorite Saarlandish restaurant in Saarbrücken, but Sandra pointed out that they didn't have too much in the way of vegetarian options.

"I'm pretty sure that by Saarlandish standards, bacon-cream sauce is vegetarian," I pointed out.

She gave me one of her looks and I consoled myself with the knowledge that Der Stiefel had a better beer selection.

We sat down and took a look at the menus. I decided on the lamb medallions with a side of spätzle noodles, and then looked around the restaurant. "Hey, check out what the waitresses are wearing." I said.

She looked up from the menu. "White shirts and aprons?"

"Yes, but look closer. They've got those same frilly collars. If you had an apron, you could go in the back and get us some food."

"Oh, you're right—not about going in the back, but about the shirt, I mean. They probably shop at the same place as I do."

"Well, if it's good enough for wait-staff, it's good enough for a philosophy professor."

"I guess. It's not like anyone at the university cares about what we wear."

"True. I feel overdressed there. My students always ask about my outfits when I show up in a tie. I tell them that a knit tie is actually less formal than not wearing a tie at all, but they look at me like I'm crazy."

"How can a tie be less formal than no tie?" She shook her head. "I agree with your students: That does sound crazy."

After dinner, we walked back to our apartment through a still-active St. Johanner Markt. Once home, Sandra hopped on the computer to check her email, I brushed my teeth, grabbed a book on English grammar, and went to the bedroom.

After finishing a chapter on the use of the subjunctive, Sandra came in the room wearing her frilly shirt, an apron, and a name tag. She was not wearing pants. She turned around to show me that she wasn't wearing underwear, either.

"Are you ready to order, sir?"

"Yes, I believe so." I managed not to laugh, but I couldn't suppress a grin.

Some time later, I lay there listening to Sandra's breathing become regular and thought about my new life in Germany. I had two part-time teaching jobs, neither of which came with any benefits and neither of which could provide me with enough money to live alone. Sandra liked to go out with her friends from work to watch football games. She didn't notice my haircuts. I occasionally spent time sewing on the machine she had given me for my birthday. We had gone out to dinner to celebrate the job even though I had wanted to stay in. And after a decent orgasm, she had fallen asleep.

I had moved to Germany to become a 1950s housewife.

Lecture Notes on Business English

Adjusting to new situations can be tough, especially if you don't speak the language. But, if Socrates can escape Plato's Cave and eventually reason about the sun, you can escape from your cubicle and eventually talk to the people around the water cooler. You just need a little help with business people and their peculiar brand of language.

It's no secret that business people are not, generally speaking, erudite wordsmiths. So, it can be difficult for those of us who paid attention in Philosophy class to interact with them after we are forced to give up our dreams and join them at staff level. But, you can do it. I believe in you. You just have to think about where you are and who you are taking to.

Like the troglodytes of old, business people don't know much about the outside world and their language reflects this. So, your first step towards effective water-cooler banter is to replace as many words as possible with furniture. Here's a few to get you started: chair, table, shelf, handle, blanket, frame, ceiling, window, bed, carpet, fork.

These words will give your speech a grounded, rational tone, which is fine for the cubicle pool, but you should aim higher. To be really impressive, add just a few words from the outside world—these will give your speech an air of sophistication and put you on the fast-track to middle management. Feel free to start with these: cloud, light, stream.

If you put it all together, no-one will suspect that you have a Thomas Wolfe novel tucked under your work-issued copy of Atlas Shrugged. Next time you are cornered, wanting nothing more than to return to your desk with your cup of organic rhubarb tea, try something like the following:

"So, the chair suggested we table the discussion because we had run into a wall trying to handle the debt ceiling handed down by management, but he was sure that if we could properly frame the issue, a window of opportunity would present itself. So I told him if we blanketed the staffroom with surveys, we would have enough data to enlighten the upper-management, then we could shelve our responsibility and finally put the issue to bed. He agreed, and liked the idea of carpeting the staffroom with surveys, but still favored forking the project so we wouldn't have to worry about how the upstream team handled the pull requests. And I told him that would work as long as we maintained cloud access."

Mmm. Can't you almost smell the breeze from an office window? A few more furniture-peppered paragraphs like that and you'll be ready to join middle management. But you're not quite ready yet.

After you master the art of dealing with office furniture's use as a language tool for office language, it's time to think about after-work situations: office parties, team-building excursions, or Kevin-from-accounting's divorce party. And the technique here is pretty simple: When you want to say how drunk someone was, take any object (but not an office furniture object lest you confuse your conversational partner), and turn it into a verb. The more exotic the object, the more drunk Jim from accounting was. Also, please note that the effect works best with an adverb. Writers might avoid adverbs, but business people respond to adverbs like road rash responds to hydrogen-peroxide: They get all bubbly.

Basic drunk: "Did you see Jim at the Christmas party? He was completely hammered."

Exotic drunk: "When Jim slid his ass off the photocopier, it hit me: We were totally tromboned."

It's often a good idea to follow up statements of drunkenness assessment, with a further statement describing the general level of bacchanalian debauchery. This can be done, strangely enough, with fruit. Nota Bene: fruit words need to be plural and need to be put into Aristotelian is-of-predication sentences to be understandable to human resources staff.

Basic debauchery: "Oh, man, how could Sandra fit so many oysters in her mouth? That was bananas." Exotic debauchery: "I couldn't believe it when Sandra showed her augmentation scars to the entire event planning team. Shit was watermelons."

Do you smell it? I smell it. It's the smell of a corner office. And it can be yours as soon as you burn your library and start using those everyday objects you find around the office as words.

The Finanzamt

Moving to any country with a functioning government will involve paperwork. And while the Germans are known for their love of bureaucracy, the paperwork involved in immigrating to the land of bratwurst and beer was mostly reasonable, so I couldn't be too annoyed by the bureaucratic hoops. I *was* annoyed by the fact that no-one at the foreign nationals office spoke a language that a foreign national might speak, however. Perhaps it was by design or perhaps it was just because Saarbücken is a rather rural city despite its state-capital status, but whatever the reason, nobody there spoke anything but German.

Luckily for me, I had Sandra to act as translator.

It didn't take long to realize that Sandra hated navigating those offices, tracking down the required forms, and procuring the right stamps even more than I did. Before we set out for the day, I'd watch her prepare. She'd look up the addresses, jot down notes, check bus times, and by the end of the process her face would set into a look of grim determination. But after a day of waiting rooms, stamped forms, and pinched-faced clerks, her eyes would become unfocused. She was somewhere else. But, the following day, the routine would repeat and we would go out to places she hated and talk to people she despised so that I could stay with her.

It must have been love.

"You know what I want to do," she said one day after a visit to an office." I want to buy a house in the forest and have no more contact with paperwork. No more taxes, no more residency permits, no more contracts."

"Can I have electricity and access to the internet at this cabin?" I asked.

"No. To get internet we'd need a contract with some company."

"Won't you need a contract to buy the cabin?"

"That's not the kind of cabin I had in mind."

"So, a stolen cabin then?"

"Just a cabin in a place without paperwork."

"So, Somalia then?"

For Sandra, it was the power-dynamics of the bureaucracy that frustrated her. The fact that people with rubber stamps had the power to make her life difficult was disturbing enough to make life in a cabin seem like a reasonable alternative.

I couldn't really blame her. I responded to the powerlessness and absurdity with my own fantasy. When faced with a clerk who wouldn't provide me with a form that I needed, I took a deep breath and imagined myself jumping over his desk and wrapping my hands around his throat. Sure, he would struggle at first, but after realizing it was hopeless to fight against someone my size, he would calm down and contemplate the decisions he had made which led him to this point in his life. And just before losing consciousness, I would see a spark of understanding in his eyes. "You know," he would think, "this guy strangling me is right. This copy of his birth certificate which was issued seven months ago is just as good as one issued in the last six months. Why do we even want new copies of birth certificates anyway? It's not like birth dates change. You can't change the past. If we could, I wouldn't be dying right now."

I took a deep breath. "So, what you are telling me is that I have to order a new birth certificate from Michigan, have it translated and stamped by an official translator, and then bring them both back here before either one is older than six months. And I have to do this even though that certificate will look exactly like the one I'm holding right now except for the date of issue."

Sandra translated for me and when the guy

answered I could tell from the tone and his face that it was pointless to stay there any longer.

"We need to get newer documents," Sandra said.

"Yeah, I gathered that much."

When we got home, Sandra curled up in a blanket with her laptop and looked at Caspar David Friedrich paintings. I caught a glimpse of a man in a desolate landscape looking out over a sea of fog. To me the painting was a mildly depressing, self-reflective piece, but I was sure Sandra thought the painting depicted a man looking for a place to build a house.

I left her to her paintings and got out my dictionary and a pen. There were still a few more forms to get and even though my German was nowhere near good enough to talk to bureaucrats, I decided to try to get at least some of the forms without Sandra's help. She had suffered enough. And besides, I liked fantasizing about strangling people, so why not go it alone?

From the documents I still needed, I assumed a tax number would be the easiest to obtain. I couldn't imagine a tax office requiring much in the way of supporting documents or even language skills. Since I was essentially saying that I wanted to give them money, I didn't imagine that getting a tax number would be any more difficult than a drunk finding a spot at a blackjack table.

After work the next day, I headed over to the local tax office, the Finanzamt. The building that housed it was, like most other buildings in downtown Saarbrücken, a humorless grey monolith. A good portion of the city had been destroyed in World War II, and after the war, it was rebuilt quickly and cheaply in the style of the time. Unfortunately, the style in 1950s Germany was unpainted concrete blocks.

The inside was about as lifeless as the outside. The front doors opened to a wall with what I took to be a directory of offices and people, but I didn't understand hardly any of it. To the left was a glass door leading to a darkened hallway and to the right a small flight of stairs leading down to a pool of cubicles. I could hear some light keyboard tapping, which suggested that at least a few of the cubicles were occupied, but it was pretty quiet considering the size of the room and the fact tile and concrete aren't the best sound dampeners.

Just in front on the cubicles a bald man with a bushy mustache sat at a raised desk, reading a magazine. After consulting my vocabulary list, I headed down and and told him that I needed a tax number.

"Vorname und Nachname," he said.

I had made a classic language learner's mistake: I had learned how to ask a question, but hadn't learned what possible answers to that question might be. I should have known better since I had seen my students make the same mistake. They could learn to ask a simple question like 'Is there a post office nearby?' and when they heard me give the book's recommended answer of, 'There's one at the end of the street,' they would do just fine. But real life is rarely as simple as a beginner's book. In fact, sometimes when I thought my students were becoming too cocksure, I would go off-script and answer in a more natural way. "Yeah, so what you have to do, you see, is get back out on the main road there and head north. After about a mile and a half you'll see the old Perkins place—it's got one of them white picket fences—you can't miss it. Just after that you'll wanna hang a right onto, I think it's Oak street, but that don't matter 'cause there ain't no sign anyway. Just hang a right after the fence and you'll see the post office after a bit. It's just past a copse of really pretty maples."

The guy looked down without pity from his raised desk. "Winston Churchill," he said a bit louder than before. "Vorname: Winston. Nachname: Churchill." He pointed at me. "Vorname. Nachname."

I nodded, impressed with his quick thinking and equally impressed that he had picked a name an English speaker would recognize. "Vorname: Robert. Nachname: McGee," I said.

"Gut." He looked down at some document on his desk. "Zweihundertsechsundzwanzig."

I shook my head and slid him my notebook. He wrote the number two hundred twenty-six in it. I said thanks and asked him where the office was. He pointed to the darkened hallway, and I thanked him again.

As soon as I opened the door to the dark hallway, the lights turned on. Just to the right of the door there was an elevator. I assumed I needed to go to the second floor and didn't really feel like looking for the stairs, so I hit the button.

Like the cubicle pool on the ground floor, the second floor was quiet. When I found the right office, I knocked and heard a small female voice telling me to enter.

Once inside, I took the offered seat and told her I needed a tax number. This was the part I had prepared for so things went smoothly; I knew how to say my address, birth-date, and employment status in German. And then she asked me what my religion was and fear set in. Not fear of God, of course, but fear that I was in the wrong place. No government official had ever asked about my religion in the States—as far as I knew they were bared from doing so by the Constitution—and since Germany seemed like a civilized, modern country I couldn't believe they would ask about it either. Didn't they have a constitution?

"Religion?" I asked hoping I had misunderstood a word that is exactly the same as the English word.

"Yes."

"I need a tax number."

"Yes. Religion?"

"Am I in the right place? Is this the Finanzamt?" After asking I realized I had switched to English.

She said something I didn't understand and then left the room.

For a moment I thought about leaving myself, but quickly realized I had just given her my name and address so leaving before I figured out what was going wrong would have been unwise. *But*, I thought, *her computer is on and I could just delete—but no, that's crazy thinking.*

The small-voiced woman came back in followed by a young man in a faded polo shirt and wrinkly khaki trousers, which wasn't an outfit I would have expected from a state bureaucrat so it did nothing to calm me down. *Who were these people?*

"So, you need a tax number," he said to me in accented but friendly English.

"Yes. Am I in the right place?"

"This is the place." He shook my hand and sat down in the chair next to me. "Ms. Becker told me you were confused by the religion question. The reason we need it is that the German state collects taxes for the church. We just need to know which church."

"Really? So if I say the Church of Rob, you'll collect taxes and give it to me?"

"No." He giggled. "It doesn't work like that. We collect for either the Catholic Church or the Evangelical Church."

I screwed up my face. "Evangelicals? Why? So they can build creationist museums?"

"No, sorry. I think I said the word wrong. How do

you call the churches that aren't Catholic? The ones from after Martin Luther."

"Protestant."

"That's right. Protestant. A strange word. We collect for the Catholics and the Protestants. They run kindergartens and other social services, and the state helps fund those projects."

"But what about the other religions? Aren't there any Muslim or Jewish kindergartens?"

"We don't collect for them."

This seemed unfair to me, but I didn't feel like having a debate about inclusive, non-demeaning civic policies with a guy who didn't iron his pants. Instead, I asked if I had to pay the church tax at all.

"No, but if you don't, it might be harder to get married in a church or send your kids to a church-run daycare centers."

Since I wasn't terribly interested in getting married by a virgin in a place with a crucified man on the wall or sending my future children to a daycare that denied the existence of dinosaurs, I told him I didn't want to pay the church tax.

He told the small-voiced woman what I had said, she made a few clicks on her computer, and then printed out my tax number form. I thanked them both and made my way out.

Once out of the Finanzamt, I made a beeline for the Diskonto Schenke, my favorite bar-disguised-as-a-restaurant in Saarbrücken. Their house specialties normally involved a heaping plate of meat-stuffed mashed potatoe dumplings smothered in bacon-cream sauce, and I loved all of the variations on that theme, but after days of dealing with the complicated pains Germany liked to inflict upon its citizens and immigrants, I was desperate for its simple pleasures: bratwurst and beer. I went up to the bartender and knew exactly what to say and what to expect. The bartender offered me some chips and I took one and then took a swig of my beer. There was comfort in the ceremony.

When I got home, I showed Sandra my newly stamped document. Clearly impressed, she smiled and added it to the growing pile on my desk. And while I might have limited our choices of daycare centers, I had done something to ease the pain of a person willing to torture herself for our life together. It was about as religious as I was willing to get.

Rome: A Travel Story

About a year after I had moved to Germany, my best friend from graduate school rang me up and told me that he would be coming to Europe. He asked if Sandra and I were interested in meeting up with him and his girlfriend, Mackenzie, in Rome. I agreed immediately and made a mental note to tell Sandra the news once she got home and hopped she hadn't already made plans for the summer.

Luckily, she hadn't made any plans that couldn't be canceled, so a few months later, we were flying over the Alps. She kept trying to get me to look out the window and be impressed with how pretty they were, but I had bought a new video game for the trip that was way better than I had expected it to be, so I couldn't muster much interest in snow-covered dirt, no matter how tall it was.

The flight didn't take us to Rome directly but to a

small town just outside the city. We had booked a hotel there rather than downtown Rome in order to save a bit of money. We still needed to find some way to get to that cheaper hotel from the airport, but we didn't expect this to be a problem. In Germany, the bus stops have maps, charts, diagrams, and time-tables which explain things pretty clearly, at least if you have some practice with the system or an advanced degree in civil engineering, and we thought Italy would be about the same.

It wasn't. The bus stop had a number and that was it. No time plan. No route plan. Just the number thirteen—a perfectly respectful title for a Johnny Cash song, but useless as bus stop.

Since we couldn't even tell when the next bus would be coming, we decided to take a taxi. I could speak English, passable German, and a little Spanish, and Sandra could speak German, English and passable French, so between the two of us, traveling through most of Europe was no problem.

We found some taxis lined up a little ways from the bus stop and went up to the first one.

"Hi, do you speak English?" I asked.

He shook his head no.

"Können Sie Deutsch?"

He shook his head nein.

"Parlez-vous français?"

And another shake for non.

"Habla español?"

And one last one for the Spanish 'no.'

I was starting to get frustrated and I was sure he could see that I was running out of languages, so he tried his best to make me feel better.

"I speak-a Italy!" The hand-pumping was a bit surprising. He was super proud to speak Italy.

"OK. Hotel Ciampino?" I asked.

"Yes, yes. Hotel Ciampino."

We put our suitcases in the trunk, me feeling stupid for not starting the conversation with the name of the destination, and got in the backseat. Fifteen minutes later we were at the hotel. It was small and a bit homely, but according to the internet it had staff that could speak English and a bar that was open late, so I wasn't disappointed.

When we went to check in, we learned that the internet had lied about the staff speaking English. I looked around hoping the internet hadn't also misled us about the bar. There were some chairs off in one corner next too a tiny bar, so I exhaled.

We managed through the language troubles and got the key. There was a stack of cards at the front desk that had the hotel's name and address on them, so I took a few. I thought that if I ran across another taxi driver who only spoke Italy, I would just give him the card.

The room was small and mostly unimpressive, but it did have one feature I was excited to try out: the wall in front of the bed was one gigantic mirror.

"Hey, Sandra, check out this mirror. You can see the whole bed. It's awesome. Why don't you take off your clothes and let's try this out."

"I'm too tired. It was a long trip." One disadvantage of having a European girlfriend is that they think traveling three hours to get somewhere is a long trip.

"It's still early. Take a shower, wake up a bit, and let's get it on."

"I think I just want to go to bed. Maybe read a bit."

"All right. Tomorrow then. I'm going to go check out the bar. Oh, you could call Jeff and see where he wants to meet tomorrow."

"Sure. I can do that. I have their hotel number in my bag."

"Cool. Then, good night, my dear."

"Night."

I grabbed a book and headed back downstairs. The bar was mostly empty. An older man was sitting in one corner with a glass of wine. I gave him a nod and put my stuff on the table furthest away from him.

The bartender was the same guy who had checked us in, so I knew English was out, but I had learned from my pre-vacation research that 'beer' is nearly the same in Italian, so that wasn't going to be a problem. I already knew how to say 'large'—decades of hanging out in coffee shops had prepared me for that much.

Beer in hand, I returned to my table and started to read. Drinking alone didn't bother me—that never bothered me. I didn't understand the stigma against drinking alone. If it's good in a crowd, it's good alone. Truthfully, it was social drinkers I didn't understand. If you need a drink to have fun with the people you are with, why hang out with them at all?

The beer was surprisingly good. I had expected it to be terrible, like the beer in France, but instead it was mild and drinkable, like the beer in America. It went down easy.

A few hours later, I stumbled up to the room. It was dark inside. I fumbled my way into the bathroom, shut the door, turned on the light, and was grateful that Sandra had gotten my toothbrush out of my bag. Brushing my teeth, I was filled with love. My drunk mind was a romantic.

Light off, I slipped back into the room and got undressed. It was too hot for pajamas—I didn't know where they were anyway. Under the sheet, I cuddled up to Sandra. Briefly. It was too hot for that, too.

***

I felt a hand on my shoulder. "Rob. Wake up."

It felt like I just just fallen asleep, but the light streaming in suggested otherwise. "What time is it?" I asked.

"9:30." Sandra was already dressed and ready to go.

"Do we have coffee?"

"I'm sure they do downstairs," she said.

"All right. Let me find pants."

"You might want to wear shorts today. It's going to be hot."

"And look like a tourist?"

"You are a tourist."

"Fair point. Where's my Panama hat?"

After coffee and a rather boring breakfast of semi-fresh bread and mild cheeses, we made our way into Rome. We bought a map at the train station and headed out to find Jeff and Mackenzie. Their hotel was pretty close to the train station, so that didn't take long.

I spotted Jeff and Mackenzie holding hands from about a block away. They could not have looked more American—bright clothes, bright smiles, and soft in all the right places.

"Oh, my God, it's so good to see you," Sandra said when we got closer.

"Cool. You found us." Jeff nodded approvingly and scratched his chin. He had grown a thin beard since I had last seen him.

Hugs all around.

"You guys look great," Sandra said.

"Thanks, you too. Nice hat," Jeff said to me.

I smiled, realizing I had missed Jeff's sarcasm.

"So, what do we want to do today?" Sandra asked.

"Let's just walk around. We've got ten days, so we don't need to rush to all of the sites," I said.

"Sounds good to me," Jeff said. "Mackenzie bought

an architectural guide book that she wants to use."

Rome was a beautiful city. One of the most impressive aspects of it was that we never knew what we would find around the corner—we would walk past a modern apartment building and then find ourselves in front of an ancient building that used to be brothel frequented by ancient Roman senators. Mackenzie filled us in on the details, and I assumed she was telling us the truth.

"Hey, Mackenzie, what's that one over there?" I asked after spotting a colossal, white marble building perched on the top of a small hill.

"Hold on, let me find it." She fumbled around for her book, tucked a lock of blonde hair behind her ear, and then pulled the book out of her bag. "OK, got it," she said after a brief search. "That one was built to honor loyalty and work."

"Why would people build something as beautiful as that to honor loyalty and work? Let's find the building that honors sex and drinking."

"I think those buildings are in Greece," Jeff said.

I nodded, tipping my ridiculous tourist hat in his direction.

After a while, we began to get hungry. Normally, I liked to avoid the tourist areas when settling down to eat, but in Rome nearly every area was a potential tourist area, so it was hard to know where to go. We eventually gave up looking for a non-tourist place and picked a pizzeria in view of the Colosseum.

At the pizzeria, we could sit outside, which was one of the reasons we picked it. It also had a few TVs mounted on stands positioned around the tables that were playing some soccer game—that was not one of the reasons we picked it.

I went up to a waiter. "English, español, oder Deutsch?"

"I speak English."

"Cool. Could we get a table for four?"

"Yes. Follow me."

We ordered drinks and took a look at the menus. I noticed that the waiter stopped on his way inside to watch the game for a bit. Just checking the score, I supposed.

The drinks came and we placed our orders. Again, the waiter stopped to watch the game for a bit before heading inside. I had been living in Europe long enough to expect poor service in restaurants, but a waiter watching a soccer game at work was still more than I could tolerate in good humor.

The pizzas were taking a while and the beers had been empty a while, so I started to scan the restaurant for the waiter. I spotted him. He was sitting at a table watching the game. I hoped that the enjoyment he got out of watching grown men feign injuries and kick a ball was greater than the enjoyment he would have gotten out of a tip, because that was the choice he had made.

The pizzas arrived and our drinkers were refilled.

Sandra closed her eyes and inhaled deeply. "These smell wonderful."

We all agreed that she was right, and barely spoke until the pizzas were gone.

When we got the bill, it seemed a bit higher than we had expected. We looked it over and called the waiter back.

"Excuse me, can you explain this charge?" I asked.

"That's for the beer," he said after a glance at the receipt.

"No. The beer is here where it says 'birra'—that word I know."

"Oh, sorry, it's for the table."

"We're not going to give you twenty euros to sit at a table. Half the time, you were watching TV and my beer was empty. I'm not giving you a tip."

"It's not a tip. It's a table fee. It's normal in Italy. But, OK, four euros. Is that OK?"

"Fine."

Outside the restaurant, I looked over at Sandra digging through her bag. "Whatcha looking for?"

"I think I remember something about these table fees from when I was here with my high school class. I want to see if the guidebook says anything about them." She leafed through her book. "OK, here it is. It says that table fees are common throughout Rome, especially in tourist areas like those around the Colosseum." She closed the book and put it back in her bag. "So, I guess that means you were an ass to that guy."

"'Ass' is a bit strong," I said, "He's the one who was watching soccer at work. Plus, he did lower the price, so we learned there is room for negotiation."

"I don't know about that. But, the book also said that many places don't charge a table fee, but those tend to have higher food prices."

"Good to know," Jeff said with a smile. "We'll go to the normal places, Rob will be an ass, we'll negotiate, and have the best of both worlds."

"Let's maybe not do that," Mackenzie said.

"I'm fine with Jeff's plan," I said.

Since it was right there, we walked over and got in line to see the Colosseum. Twenty minutes later, we were in, but it was less impressive than the outside, which was gorgeous. I had expected to see floor of the arena, but it was missing. Instead, we could look down into the empty rooms that were under where the arena floor used to be. These rooms were where the gladiators, slaves and animals were kept when they weren't trying to kill each other up above. Interesting to be sure, but you can only spend so much time looking at empty rooms before it all starts to look the same. We eventually got bored and headed back out into the city.

"So, where to next?" Mackenzie asked.

"Let's get a bottle of wine and hang out in a park," I said. "Or we could grab a drink and then check out that Foro Romano place."

"I'm up for the wine plan," Jeff said. "We can do the Foro Romano tomorrow."

"Cool. Mackenzie? Sandra? Wine in a park?" I said.

They agreed and we set out to find a grocery store. It didn't take long to find one and while we were there, Sandra suggested we get some food for dinner later—bread, cheese, antipasti. A little picnic. It sounded nice, but I suspected she just wanted to keep me out of restaurants for a little while.

I bought two bottles of wine.

We spent the rest of the day in the park, which was lovely. When it started to get dark, we decided to head back to our hotels. So, after dropping Jeff and Mackenzie off at their hotel we headed up the road to the train station. We checked the schedule and saw that our train would be leaving in five minutes. Perfect timing. We walked over to the platform and saw that our train was already moving.

Sandra was furious. "What kind of trains leave early?"

"It's OK," I said. "We'll just take the next one."

"There is no next one. That was the last one until five o'clock tomorrow morning."

"OK, so we take a taxi. It's no big deal. I've got cards with the hotel's address on them. We're good." I really didn't understand why she was so upset. Maybe early trains were offensive to Germans.

We got a taxi in front of the train station and made it back to the hotel. Inside, Sandra told me she was going to take a shower, and I started to get my hopes up. I thought about joining her in there, but decided against it, thinking she wanted to relax a bit after missing the train.

When she came out, I hopped out of bed and grabbed some clean clothes. "Don't start without me." I said as she walked past me.

She got into bed and opened a book.

When I got out, she was already sleeping, glasses still on. I threw on some pants and went downstairs to the bar.

***

The next day, we skipped our hotel's breakfast and met Jeff and Mackenzie at their hotel for theirs. When we walked in, they were talking to their front desk clerk, who spoke perfect English, about interesting stuff to do in and around the city. Mackenzie took us up their room and we sat on their balcony. Their room was tiny, more like a closet than a room, but the balcony was a nice perk. It overlooked an alley, which might not sound like much, but alleys don't get much traffic, so, really, it was about as good as one might expect in the middle of a big city—especially a big city like Rome, which is not known for its calm, respectful drivers.

Jeff joined us a short while later with a pot of coffee and breakfast. He gave Mackenzie a kiss and sat down. They were especially cuddly with each other, apparently having had a more romantic night than I'd had.

I poured myself a cup of coffee and grabbed a slice of ciabatta.

"So, did the front desk guy have any good tips?" Sandra asked.

"Yeah, he told me about this place not too far from here called Ostia Antica. It used to be a port city, but was abandoned. I guess because it's not on the coast anymore. It was rediscovered and excavated in the early twentieth century and is well preserved. Apparently, the mosaics and frescoes are really impressive."

"That sounds great," Sandra said.

"What's a fresco?" I asked.

"It's a painting on a wall." Sandra informed me with a touch of playful condescension.

"So, it's like ancient graffiti? A Roman Banksky? That sounds pretty cool."

"So, do you want to go?" Sandra asked.

I put down the coffee cup. "No."

"Well, what do *you* want to do?"

"I want to go to the beach."

"I'm not so interested in the beach," Jeff said. "I'm from California. I've seen beaches."

"I grew up on the beach, too," I replied. "But the beachgoers in Michigan aren't as pretty as the Italians. And, more importantly, Europeans aren't so shy with their nudity." I turned to Mackenzie. "Help me out here, Kenz. Old graffiti or naked Italians?"

"I'm leaning toward graffiti."

"But, you love the naked. I've seen your book collection." Mackenzie was a big fan of art that blurred the smut/art line—the work of Robert Mapplethorpe, early twentieth-century pin-ups, Ronald Reagan's autobiography—nasty stuff.

We went to Ostia Antica. It was actually pretty cool despite the fact the only nudity was in the frescos.

The train ride home was full of all of the beachgoers that I had wanted to see, and they were beautiful. A girl next to us was still in beach-party mode and kept bouncing around, dancing to music that wasn't there anymore. She was like something out of a Russ Meyer movie and I tried hard not to stare, but she was still glistening with tanning oil and despite the tiny bikini top I couldn't see any tan-lines. It was torture.

At the train station back in Rome, we made plans for the following day. Jeff suggested Vatican City. Sandra had been there before and wasn't interested in seeing it again, but said we should just go without her because it was worth seeing once. I didn't object.

On the train back to Campino, Sandra made a point of telling me how tired she was and how nice it would be to take a shower and then go to sleep. It wasn't exactly what I wanted to hear. I thought about pressing the issue, but knew it was pointless; this wasn't the first time vacationing had interrupted bedroom activities. On our last trip she asked me in the airport if I had remembered to turn off the coffee pot. I was sure I had until she asked, then the doubt set in. She stressed about that coffee pot the entire time we were in the States. I wasn't sure what the problem was here in Rome. I suspected it had something to do with being in a busy city rather than camping in the mountains, but I also suspected that knowing the cause of the stress wouldn't have made anything less frustrating.

When we got back to the hotel, she went up to the room and I went to the bar.

***

The next morning hit hard. The shiny metal coffee pot in the hotel lobby reflected eyes red and raw. I drank the first cup standing in front of the machine and grabbed another for the road. When the train arrived in Rome, I was almost back to my normal self, so I had one more coffee to complete the project and then went downstairs to find the subway to Vatican City.

The ceilings were a bit low down there.

At six foot four, I was moderately tall by American standards. Back home in southern Germany, I was an impressive sight. But in Rome, I was a god. At least that's what I was thinking while I was waiting for the subway. The platform was packed—the crowd stretched for as far as I could see in both directions— hundreds of people, not one of which was taller than my nipples.

The trip wasn't long, which was good since there were far too many people in the car for my tastes. I tried to distract myself from the oppressive group by concentrating on a few of the more attractive members. One businessman wore a beautiful tan suit that caught my eye, and a woman standing next to the door caught my eye more than once. I didn't stare of course. But a few furtive glances did pass the time.

When I left the station, I looked around for another place to get a coffee and maybe a croissant to calm the coffee which had been jostling around inside my stomach.

I spotted a café across the street, and immediately after ordering, I realized that my wallet was gone.

Panic set it. My mind ran though possibilities: Had I forgotten it? No. I had bought train tickets. Had I lost it? Unlikely. I hadn't put it down anywhere.

It had been stolen.

Had the woman in the train been a distraction? No, that was just paranoia talking.

I was starting to hate Italy.

Not sure what to do and with the appointment to meet Jeff and Mackenzie in mind, I wandered over to the Vatican Museums, found Jeff and Mackenzie, and told them what had happened.

We all agreed that I should file a police report in case the thief decided to use my credit cards, but we also agreed that that was unlikely so it would probably be OK to check out the museums first so we didn't lose our place in line. The line was, after all, long enough to convince me that the pain of reversing charges on a stolen credit card was less than the prospect of ending up at the end of the museum line.

The museums were gigantic and we knew we didn't want to spend all day in there, so we made a plan to hit the highlights. I spent most of time looking at marble statues, wishing the medieval Christians hadn't been so prude. The fact they thought a hastily plastered-on fig leaf was less offensive than a penis, showed how short-sighted they were. How was it those fig leaves were being held up? Well, like every man, I'd held up a towel before, so I knew the mechanics well despite never having tried to hold up a leaf.

When we were ready to leave, we followed a crowd to the Sistine Chapel, found a few seats and looked up at what just might have been the world's most beautiful ceiling. The room was full and the noise got steadily louder until the guards started telling people to be quiet in various languages. The crowd would then quiet, but then, like a classroom without a competent teacher, it would get steadily louder until the guards would start the quieting process once again. This repeated every five minutes.

We left through the back and with the help of a passerby, found a police station. Inside, I told the officer what had happened. He didn't speak English, so he went to get another officer. I wasn't sure why he didn't stop me before I had finished my story. When the other officer arrived, I asked if he spoke English, and after he nodded, I told the story again. With a wave, he directed me to follow him into a back room.

We sat around a little table and the English-speaking officer pulled a form out of a filling cabinet and handed it to me. After walking me through the form, he asked me to call Missouri to report the stolen IDs, but I told him that Missouri was seven hours behind Italy and they wouldn't be in the office for another hour or so.

He started yelling at the other officer, who yelled back, even cupping his hand around his mouth so that his yells would carry over the small table. It was a fascinating way to communicate and I couldn't stop smiling.

We finished up the form and went back to the lobby. Jeff and Mackenzie were talking to an elderly American couple who had also been victims of theft. Someone had slit the side of the woman's purse open and took her wallet. She hadn't even noticed until they went to pay for lunch. After listening to her story, I felt lucky. At least my thief hadn't stabbed me in the ass to get my wallet.

We had a few hours before we were supposed to meet Sandra for dinner, so we headed over to St. Peter's Basilica. Mackenzie wanted to see Michelangelo's Pietà and I wanted to climb to the top of the dome to look out over Rome and imagine it on fire.

Once inside, I convinced Jeff and Mackenzie to climb up to the top with me. We opted for the cheaper stair route rather than the elevator, but it was a long way to the top and my legs were burning by the time we got there. And then Mackenzie lost her nerve.

"I don't want to go out there," she said, starring out the open door which lead to a thin path which curved around the outside of the dome.

"What are you talking about?" I asked. "It'll be cool."

"I'm afraid it will fall."

"This thing has survived two world wars and a German Pope. It's not going to fall because a *kräftig* American walks out on the balcony."

"What does that mean?"

"It means you are beautiful and I love you. So, let's get out there and pretend to be the Pope."

Jeff took her by the hand and they walked out.

The city looked great from up there even though it wasn't on fire.

***

When we got back into Rome we met up with Sandra and found a restaurant away from the obvious tourist places. The people inside looked to be well-dressed Italians, there wasn't a single pair of cargo shorts in sight which would have indicated Americans, so we thought it was worth a try.

We were all pretty hungry, and everything on the menu sounded excellent, so we were having a hard time deciding. We knew we wanted to order two appetizers, but we weren't sure which two. Stuffed zucchini blossoms? Roasted artichokes? Shrimp and rosemary crostini? There were eight options and each one we discussed sounded better than the last. The waiter came up while we were debating.

"Can't decide what to get?" His English was pretty good, and his hands remained inactive. Maybe he was a foreigner.

"All of the appetizers sound wonderful," Sandra answered.

"It's a no problem. I bring you a sample platter and you can try everything."

"That's sounds great; let's do that. Sound good, guys?" Mackenzie said.

We agreed and ordered some drinks. The waiter left and we looked over the main courses. When he returned with our drinks, we ordered our main courses. He buzzed off once again and was back almost immediately with the appetizers, which seemed like a lot of food.

"These are amazing," Mackenzie said between bites.

Sandra started messing with her glasses.

"What's wrong?" I asked.

"My glasses keep slipping. I think I bent them when I fell asleep with them on the other night."

"Do you need them to eat?" Mackenzie asked.

"Oh, God, yes," I replied. "She's blind without glasses. But she doesn't normally wear them to bed, so, now that I think about it, I don't think she's ever seen me naked. When we have sex, I might as well be a stranger."

"I don't need to see you," Sandra replied, "I just need to smell you." She smiled in my direction—we both knew how much of a fan she was of smells—but I wanted the conversation to end. Not because it was in front of our friends, but because it reminded me of how long it had been.

I looked at my food.

Another bottle of wine later, the waiter arrived with the bill and we saw why the appetizers seemed like a lot of food. He hadn't brought a sample platter, he had brought one order of all of them and charged us full price for each. At about eight euros per appetizer, dinner, the bread we'd thought was free, and drinks, the bill has high, and I was furious. Again.

"Sandra, does your guidebook have Italian phrases in it?" I asked.

"Yeah, some."

"How do I say, 'Rome would be a nice city if it didn't have Romans in it'?"

"Let's just go."

When we got back to Ciampino, it was still early so I asked Sandra if she wanted to take a walk before going upstairs. "It might make us feel better," I said. She said she wanted to do some reading. I gave her a kiss, watched her go inside, and then took a walk around the neighborhood.

When I got back to the room I noticed that Sandra had forgotten to draw the curtains. The light from the street illuminated the bed. She was in one of my t-shirts sleeping on her stomach. One leg was stretched out straight, but the other was pulled up, which prevented the t-shirt from covering anything below her hips. She wasn't wearing underwear.

A few days later we met Jeff and Mackenzie for breakfast. Their flight was that evening, and we wanted to squeeze in a few more sights before they had to pack and leave.

We didn't really have a plan, so we just wandered around a neighborhood we hadn't been to yet. We sat on some steps which were apparently famous and drank a few beers. We then walked over to a fountain which was also apparently famous and threw in some coins. The local story was that if you threw a coin into the fountain, you would one day return to Rome. I took a picture of Sandra as she threw her coin and managed to capture the coin in the shot—the sun reflected off of it at just the right moment.

We had an ice cream and had to say our goodbyes.

After a hug from Jeff and a cheek-kiss from Mackenzie, it was time for them to go.

Sandra and I decided to head back to explore

Ciampino a bit. Get a taste of non-Roman Italy. It was mostly a residential city with little in the way of sights, but was nice enough. As dinner time approached, we started looking for a place to eat. Heading back to our hotel, we spotted a place with quite a few motorcycles parked out front and a small group of leather-glad bikers drinking beer. We could hear live music playing inside.

A biker bar in Italy. We couldn't resist.

We went inside and asked if they served food. They did, so we got a table. We ordered sandwiches and beer and enjoyed the sights. It was strange. Being in a biker bar surrounded leather jackets, tattoos, and exposed midriffs was the first time in Italy I didn't feel like someone was trying to rip me off. It felt like home in some strange way. Sandra looked to be enjoying herself as well.

The drinks came, the food came, the music was loud. Sandra smiled.

We finished our sandwiches and listened.

"Should we get another round?" I asked.

"No. Let's go back to the room. It's been too long."

I waved for the waitress while Sandra dug around for her wallet. The waitress appeared and said something I didn't understand. I nodded. Sandra gave her thirty euros, a smile, and a 'buona notte,' and we were outside.

Back in the room, hands were everywhere. We tangled up in front of the mirror.

It was glorious.
I could see everything.

Dogs Can't Eat Chocolate, but They Are Pretty Good at Logic

Yesterday was hot and I wanted ice cream. Like most German cities, mine has its fair share of ice cream parlors. There is the new trendy place that refuses to use ice cream scoops and thinks cilantro belongs in a waffle cone, and there are the Italian places that, for the low price of all of your money, will serve you elaborate arrangements of ice cream and fruit that taste like heaven despite looking like funeral arrangements.

But I was feeling nostalgic. I needed something artificial and too sweet. A taste of home. A chemistry experiment masquerading as food.

I wanted a McDonald's sundae.

That fudge-filled desire outweighed my desire to remain pants-less in front of a fan, so I headed downtown. Once inside, I took in the grease smells of my childhood and, smiling, approached the counter manned by a woman with more eye makeup than Ronald himself. "Hi, I'd like a sundae with caramel sauce, please," I said in my best German.

"Pardon?"

"Sundae. Caramel sauce." A bit slower that time.

"Once more?"

It seemed my accent was causing problems, so I tried a few alternative pronunciations. "Cara-mel sauce? Car-mul sauce?"

With an apologetic grimace, she shook her head.

A strategy switch was in order. I thought back on my college days in logic class. When the professor wasn't screaming at us, he had pretty good advice. One day, after the screaming, he threw his chalk on the floor and told us in the sweetest voice he could manage through clenched teeth that even dogs understood disjunctive syllogisms.

I hoped fast-food employees were as rational as dogs.

I held up my hands. "You've got two kinds of sundae sauce here." I looked from one hand to the other to illustrate the choices. "Caramel and chocolate." I gave the hands alternating, emphasizing shakes. "I don't want chocolate." I put my left hand down. "I want the other one."

Her eyes widened with understanding and she nodded. "Oh, cara-MEL sauce." She hit a button on her screen and looked back up. "Anything else for you today?"

"No. Thank you." I shook my head and grinned, happily barking in my head.

Making More Germans

I didn't move to Germany to see more of the world or teach English to business people. I moved to Germany to make babies. In truth, I had tried to make babies in the States, but that girlfriend decided she'd rather move back to her hometown and be a waitress without babies instead of sticking with me and being a yoga instructor with babies. So, that didn't work out, and it was probably for the best.

When I met Sandra, I was just coming out of the relationship with said yoga instructor and wasn't thinking about babies; I was thinking about other things I wouldn't be having for the foreseeable future. I knew Sandra would be moving back to Germany at the end of the school year, so when she expressed romantic interest, I figured a year-long fling with an exchange student was a good way to fill the yoga gap.

As the school year got closer to the end, Sandra

started to have second thoughts.

"What's going to happen after I go back next month?" she asked one day while we were laying in bed, the air conditioner doing nothing to make Missouri's summer bearable.

"What do you mean?"

"I mean about us."

"Well, that will be the end of us, won't it? I mean, we talked about this at the beginning. We can have some fun for the school year, but after the winter semester, we have sex in the airport parking lot, you get on your plane, and we go on with our lives. That was the plan, right?"

"Yes, I remember the plan." She shook her head. "I don't remember the parking lot part, but yeah, that was the idea. But I want to change the plan. I think we should try to stay together."

I propped up on an elbow and looked at her for the first time in the conversation. "How could that work? I've got another year here at least. Maybe two."

"I don't know. Maybe it won't work, but there's no reason not to try. If it doesn't work, then fine, but we should at least try. We won't lose anything by trying."

"I'm not sure." I looked away and smiled. "One of my students this semester is a stripper, and I was thinking about calling her once the semester is over and she isn't my student anymore. So, I would lose that." I lay back down and starred at the ceiling.

"Can you be serious? I'm being serious. We should

try."

"Just because I joke around, it doesn't mean I'm not serious."

"OK, then what then?"

"Yeah, let's try. But the parking lot part of the plan stays."

And so we tried. It wasn't too bad, actually. Per request, once she was back in Germany, I sent her packages of my sweaty shirts so she could smell me when she slept, and she sent me nude self-portraits so I could have some images to attach to the voice during our phone calls. Plus, the German university semester is on a much different schedule from the American system, so the way it worked out was that every three months one of us would be on vacation and could fly over to the other. After a bit more than a year of that arrangement, I decided I would give up my career as a philosopher to move to Germany, under the condition that she would make some babies, and provide me with more self-portraits. The sweaty t-shirts were no longer necessary since I could sweat in person.

Organizing the trans-Atlantic move was time-consuming, but manageable. I shipped my computer, video game consoles, and a few other essentials to Germany, while my father drove down from Michigan to pick up the things I couldn't afford to ship but also couldn't bear to part with—comics, guitar, philosophy books, my collection of retro Playboy magazines.

For what remained, I held a yard sale to get rid of

everything suitable to sell in my front yard. My roommate, Jeff, took the rest of the stuff off my hands—he seemed excited to try out the swing with his new girlfriend. And that was that. I finished grading my final stack of philosophy papers, and flew to Germany.

***

It took a few months to get settled. The rumors I had heard about Germany's love of bureaucracy turned out to be true. The rumors I had heard about Germany's organized efficiency turned out to be very far from the stereotype, but this, at times, ended up working to my advantage. Many of the bureaucrats didn't know what they were doing and were easily convinced that I knew what I was doing. I didn't blame them; it was obvious that the rules were too complicated for any human to keep in mind. So, I did my research on the rules that applied to my situation, showed up in a suit, acted like I knew what I was talking about, told them which documents I needed, and assured them they could provide them to me. More often than not, they were happy that I had done their job for them.

After about a year in Germany, I had all of my paperwork in order, work was going fine, and knew I wasn't going to be deported, so I started to press Sandra about her end of the bargain: making babies.

"I'm not sure I can do it," she said.

I lowered my eyes. "You're putting me in a difficult

position here. I quit my job, sold my stuff, and moved to a new country to start a family."

"I know. It's just that now I'm not sure."

"Well, what's the worry?"

"I don't know. I like how things are now. I don't know how it will be with a baby. It sounds silly, but I'm not sure I want to share you yet."

"That's cute of you to say, and I like how things are now, too, but..." I hesitated. I didn't want to give an ultimatum, but I wasn't sure how to continue the conversation. I wasn't about to give in, but I knew enough about Sandra's personality to know that an ultimatum would be a very bad idea. I wanted to say, 'If you don't want a baby, I'll go back to the States and you'll never see me again,' but I knew that would be the wrong thing to say. The problem was, that was the only sentence rolling around in my head.

"Well, maybe you can tell my what it will be like?" she asked.

Sandra hadn't had any experience with babies, so I understood her trepidation. Consistent with German statistics, none of her friends had children, and even though her brother was older, he was happily childless as well. I, on the other hand, had had lots of experience. My sister was born when I was fourteen, so I knew all about fontanelles, diapers, teething, weak necks, projectile vomiting, and choking dangers.

I did not tell Sandra about these things.

Instead, I told her about how babies smelled, how

they fell asleep on my chest after I sang them Bob Dylan songs, and how their little fingers were so small and fragile and would grasp my finger as if it were the most important thing in the world. I told her about how their tiny lips would purse before they cried and you couldn't help but kiss them, how soft their skin was, and how they would raise their arms and beg to be hugged when a family member entered the room.

I don't know which part of my story convinced her, but she was, after a few days to think it over nevertheless convinced. We decided to continue being safe in the bedroom until the summer was over, and then be unsafe. Come what may. And so, at the end of August, I threw away everything that might hinder the baby-making project: various latex items, spermicidal gels, and more than a few pair of granny-panties.

I came home from work one day in October and was surprised to see Sandra in the kitchen. "What are you doing home?" I asked.

"My boobs felt weird, so I came home to take a pregnancy test."

"And?"

"I'm pregnant." When the words came out, whatever serious expression she was trying to maintain faltered and a smile broke through.

"Wow, that was fast. I thought it would take a few months at least." I put my bag down. Sandra stood up and came in for a hug. She pressed her head into my chest. I could feel her boobs somewhere north of my waist, but they didn't feel weird to me.

"So, since you're home, you wanna try to make twins?"

"That's not how that works, but OK. Let me take a shower first. The bus was hot. And I just peed on a stick."

***

For the most part, the pregnancy passed without issue. For me, anyway. Occasionally, once the belly expanded, Sandra would come home and complain about the hot buses, but she had often complained about those before, so that wasn't much of a change. The only difference was that in addition to the uncomfortable temperatures, the pregnant belly attracted uncomfortable social situations. She told me that strangers would sometimes ask to feel her belly, and this, understandably, made her furious. The first few times it had happened, she politely declined, but as the requests piled up, her diplomacy failed.

"So I said, 'No, you can't feel my belly. Why would you ask that? Can I feel your fat belly? Can I run my fingers through your thinning hair?' and then he got all hurt and indignant and I got off at my stop."

"You might want to be careful with that strategy," I said. "I'm sure some guys would love it if a pregnant woman rubbed them in public. I've seen videos on the internet that start that way."

"Gross. Why does that exist?"

"I don't know. I guess because everything exists on the internet. Did you know there are fetish videos of woman eating and crying?"

"That's sick. It's such a horrible feeling: being upset and hungry."

"I know, right? Can you imagine?" I made some jerking motions. "Oh, yeah, baby, but no desert for you. That salad is enough."

"Can we talk about something else?"

"Yeah, sure." I picked up a pen and smiled. "Should we make dinner plans?"

She gave me the look that meant she was done joking around and I needed to make a shopping list.

A few weeks later the due date passed without even the faintest rumble or dilation (I checked). Then another week passed without any downstairs progress, so the midwife from the prenatal course gave Sandra a drink which was supposed to inspire the baby to be more proactive. According to Sandra, the drink tasted like apricot vodka.

About an hour after the drink, the first contractions began. We hung out in our apartment for a while watching TV, and when the contractions increased in strength and frequency, we took a bus to the hospital. I had suggested a taxi, but Sandra felt confident we had plenty of time and there was no reason to spend extra money on a taxi.

Nobody on the bus asked to touch Sandra's belly. I

wasn't sure if it was because I was there or because the contractions made her face take on a murderous expression.

By the time we got to the hospital, the contractions had stopped, which was nice because the closest bus stop was at the bottom of the hill the hospital sat on and we still had a bit of a climb ahead of us. I asked Sandra if she wanted to stop off at the pub for another apricot vodka and was answered by a murderous expression not inspired by a contraction.

We signed in at the hospital and a nurse with obviously-dyed magenta hair showed us to our room and instructed Sandra to put on the hospital pajamas, which looked to be quite comfortable—much better than those ass-to-the-wind things American hospitals gave out. The nurse said she would be right back and then left, I assumed this was to give Sandra some changing privacy, but since there was another pregnant lady in the room and no curtains to hide behind, privacy wasn't a possibility anyway.

A short while late the magenta nurse returned pushing a machine, the real reason she had left. Once hooked up, the machine told the nurse that Sandra was not in labor at all, so our presence was a bit confusing. Sandra explained that she was two weeks overdue and had, on the advice of a midwife, taken the apricot vodka drink that seemed to get the process started. The nurse nodded and said she wanted to do a few more tests and then she would consult with the doctor who would then walk us through various pregnancy-starting options.

After the tests, she told us there was a little private park just outside and we should take a walk because it would be a little while before the doctor could review the results and sit down with us. Plus, "Sometimes physical activity can inspire the uterus to action," she said with a kindly smile.

When we got back inside from our park walk, the nurse met us in the hall. "Oh, good. I was just coming out to get you. The doctor is on his way."

We thanked her and went to the room to wait.

The doctor walked us through a few options, and since Sandra didn't want to have a Cesarean without first trying to have a natural birth, the doctor recommend that she get a good night's sleep before trying to induce labor. This seemed like reasonable advice, so we decided that Sandra would stay at the hospital for the night and I would return early the next morning. The doctor said I could stay as well, but Sandra didn't think it was necessary—the beds weren't big enough for the both of us and there wasn't much to do aside from watch TV, so I might as well come back in the morning.

On the way home, I stopped by the gas station and picked up a six-pack of beer, a sandwich that had seen better days, and a bag of chips I was sure I would hate because the Germans insisted on only making three kinds of chips: paprika, salt, and cheese.

Somewhere around my fifth beer and my fourth episode of *Leave It to Beaver*, the phone rang.

"I need you," Sandra said in a strained voice. "The contractions have started again. Much stronger than before. I don't want to do it alone."

I told her I was on my way, and then hung up to call a taxi, which showed up almost immediately. Like decent Japanese food, responsive taxis are one of the advantages of living in a city.

I never felt comfortable riding in the back of a taxi—felt too much like I was pretending to be rich—so I pointed to the front seat and when the driver nodded, I hopped in. The smell of alcohol was pretty strong inside the car, but I wasn't sure if it was the driver or if I was just smelling myself in the new, smaller environment.

"So, where to?" the driver asked.

"The hospital in Dudweiler."

"I'm not sure where that is."

"Dudweiler is near Scheidt, a bit north of the university."

He smiled. "Yeah, I know where that is, but not the hospital."

"Oh, uh, sorry. If you can get me to the main bus stop by the pedestrian zone, I can find it from there."

He threw his arm over the seat, looked back, and pulled out of the drive. "I'm sure there are signs. We can follow those."

"Yeah, that should work."

"So what brings you to Germany?" They could always hear my accent.

"I came here to make German babies."

H giggled. "Yeah, we could use some more of those." And he was right. I wasn't sure why Germans were so baby-adverse—Germany seemed like a good place to have kids. High standard of living, free education, some of the cheapest food in the Western world, and lots of excellent beers for the parents to choose from when the kids decided to draw big red X's on the expensive business stationary, or threw their keys in the toilet—both of which I felt bad about doing well into adulthood.

When we got to Dudweiler, the driver followed the signs to the hospital so I didn't have to climb the hill in the dark. Not that I would have minded a bit of exercise to work out the beer, but all things considered, it was better to get there sooner rather than later.

I paid him and threw in a few euros extra for some more beer. He thanked me, and I went inside.

The front desk was empty and I didn't feel like waiting, so I went directly to Sandra's room. The Germans were a trusting people. I didn't imagine too many hospitals in the States would allow clearly drunk people to wander in from the street and into the ward were the new babies were kept.

"I made it," I said, perhaps to loudly, upon entering the room.

"Oh, good," Sandra said, "but keep it down, the other mom is sleeping."

I looked over at the other bed. The woman from earlier was still there but her pregnant belly wasn't. "Oh, yeah, right. Sorry. So, what's the news?"

"The contractions are regular, and painful, but my cervix won't dilate. They keep coming in and checking this machine. I don't know what the plan is."

A short while later, a young nurse came in a checked the monitor, grimaced, and left. Almost immediately, the magenta nurse from earlier came in and checked the monitor. She also grimaced and then started pushing rather aggressively on Sandra's belly while she watched the monitor. "The baby's heart rate has slowed down. She might just be sleeping, but we need to call the doctor," she said.

Sandra and I nodded and exchanged glances. The nurse ripped the printout from the monitor and left.

A short while later, she came back in and explained that she had shown the doctor the printout and he had said that Sandra needed to have an emergency C-section. She handed me a form and told me that if I wanted to be in the room, I would need to sign it. I tried to read it, but it was difficult to concentrate on a foreign language at the time, so I just signed it and hoped I hadn't just agreed to give the baby up for adoption. The nurse then lowered Sandra's bed, pulled up some rails on the side, and pushed her out of the room. I followed them into the hall and then into an elevator.

When we got out, an older nurse with cat-eye glasses came up to us and looked at me. "I'm sorry, but we are a bit short on staff and you can't go in."

"But I signed the form," I said.

"I know, but the doctor doesn't want you in there unless there is an extra nurse for you, and we don't have an extra nurse."

"I'll be fine. I've seen a C-section before. On the big screen even." And that was true. I had taken a human growth and development class at university to fulfill a science requirement and we had spent one day watching births—natural, C-section, breach, everything. It was a bit disturbing actually; the screen in the lecture hall made everything too big—nobody needs to watch a two-foot baby head squeeze out of an unkempt three-foot vagina.

"I'm sorry." She looked like she understood, but there was nothing she could do. She motioned to a bench.

I nodded and started to make my way over to sit down when I heard Sandra call out, "Don't leave me without saying goodbye," and I felt like an asshole. I had been so focused on what I was supposed to do to make Sandra more comfortable that when it was clear I wouldn't get to do anything, I had resigned to just waiting. I hadn't even considered that Sandra also wanted me to be there, and was probably more than a little bit worried.

"I'm sorry," I said. "I'll see both of you soon." I gave her a kiss, and the nurses pushed her away.

I sat on my bench and listened to the activity in the other room. It was quiet for a while and then I heard a baby crying. I realized that this meant that Sandra had been cut open and she was currently lying in there with a sizable gash in her lower abdomen—I had seen the videos after all. It was hard for me to care about the baby when I pictured Sandra in her current state.

A few minutes later, the doctor came out. He smiled broadly and held out his hands like a fisherman describing an impressive catch. "You have a great daughter," he said in English.

It was nice of him to try to speak English to me. I did appreciate it, but I was an English teacher, so I couldn't just turn off the part of my brain that listened for mistakes. And confusing 'great' for 'big' was a common one for German speakers, so I had to try hard not to explain the misstep to him. "How is Sandra?" I asked.

"Oh, she's fine." He seemed a little surprised I was asking about Sandra instead of asking about the baby. "Your daughter will be out soon with one of the nurses. I have to go back and finish up."

"Thank you."

The cat-eye nurse who hadn't let me in the room came out smiling, pushing a hospital crib. "Here she is. Congratulations."

And there she was. A bit purple. A bit upset. I wanted to pick her up, wrap her in my arms, and fall asleep for a week.

"Come with me," the nurse said. "We need to wash her and do a check up."

"Lead the way," I said.

We got back in the elevator and went down to the maternity ward. In a room near the nurses station, she took my daughter out on the crib and gave her a bath, weighed her, felt around inside her mouth, and wrote down something on a clip board. My new girl didn't like any of this.

"Take off your shirt and have a seat," the nurse said.

"Yeah, do you think the baby's hungry?"

She giggled. "Probably, but we'll wait for your wife for that. Babies like the feel of skin."

"Who doesn't?"

I threw my shirt over the back of the chair and took a seat. Finally, the nurse gave me my daughter; she calmed down almost immediately. And then the nurse took a picture which prompted a spasm of shock and a rather loud cry from the little thing.

"Well, she's not blind," I said. I smiled at the thought. Everything seemed to be working just fine. She calmed down again, snuggled into my chest, and fell asleep. I kissed her head, thought about Sandra, and was sure she wouldn't mind sharing me with this new German girl.

I Like German When It Doesn't Make Me Think about Dead Babies

I once read that English is in the unique position amongst languages of having both imported and exported the most words. I knew we had a lot of French words, and that everyone in the world seemed to understand 'OK' so I didn't question the article. No doubt most of the sharing grew out of convenience or even laziness, but that doesn't stop me from teasing my German friends by telling them English *had* to import 'schadenfreude' because the concept of taking pleasure in someone else's misfortune would be so alien to English speakers, they would've never named it without help from the Germans.

English speakers being what they are, didn't take 'schadenfreude' without returning in kind, so they gave the Germans 'babies.' There was a different word in Germany before, of course, but take one look at 'Säuglinge' and you can guess why the birthrate has remained so low for so long. *You want to put what inside me?* I remain optimistic, but only time will tell if 'babies' can improve Germany's population troubles.

For a person learning a language, it is nice that some vocabulary is shared, as it reduces a bit of the work. Sure, I still have to know enough German grammar to know where in the sentence I have to put the 'doppelgänger,' but at least I don't have to learn the word because I learned that one when I was eight and my father thought *Invasion of the Body Snatchers* was an appropriate film for a slumber party. It wasn't, by the way, and I would like to here, again, to apologise to my mother for causing trouble with the neighbors by smashing their watermelons.

Neighbors and their pod-people aside, where things get troublesome for me in Germany is when they invent their own English-sounding words and then mistakenly use those same words when the speak to me in English. Unsurprisingly, the chances I might understand an English-sounding German word that doesn't exist in English are about as good as the chances I'd understand an English-sounding alien word. What I do understand is how German speakers might be confused—many of these new words do indeed sound English so it's easy to think they are, but, like Madonna taught us in the early 2000s, you need to do more than sound English to be English.

The classic example from this vocabulary category is 'handy,' which is the English-sounding word

I Like German When...

Germans gave cell phones—or, as Madonna probably calls them, mobile phones. And, I have to admit, 'handy' does make a little sense in so far as it can mean *useful* when it's used as an adjective—cell phones are certainly handy, no doubt about that. The problem crops up when it's used as a noun.

Where I'm from, a handy is something truckers pay prostitutes for at the rest stop, and since I've never worked in logistics, I hadn't had one since I was in high school. Now, a dry handy from a girlfriend who hasn't yet worked up the bravery to involve a mouth is nothing to complain about, but after experiencing how saliva can improve things, there's little reason to be nostalgic. So, when a shop girl overheard me speaking English with Sandra and asked, "Can I interest you in a handy?" you can forgive me when I said, "Here? In front of everyone?"

When Sandra and I found the kids clothing department, I found an even more disturbing lexical misstep. There, amongst the tiny socks and pointless running shoes, I found the t-shirts we were looking for. Macabrely, the Germans had named them 'bodies.' Not bodysuits, mind, simply: bodies. The babies pictured on the packaging looked lively enough, but being labeled as 'bodies,' like some post-modern art exhibit's attempt to shock, meant I couldn't look beyond their cute, toothless smiles and see anything other than their mortality.

While it's no doubt true that I might, at times, be

a bit rough around the edges, the prospects of buying clothes which used dead babies as mascots did give me pause.

I'm sure I would have eventually forgotten about the shopping trip, but as we were making our way to the cashier, a display etched the trip into my brain. "New and on Sale: Body Bags!"

They weren't actually body bags, of course, but misnamed backpacks, which in itself was strange since quite a few English speakers are happy using the German work 'rucksack.'

I turned to Sandra. "Every big city in Germany has at least one language school like mine with native English speakers on staff. Why don't these companies schedule a lesson and check to make sure their made-up words aren't insane? I would have more clients and they could prevent their employees from offering hand jobs and dead babies. Everyone would win. Especially the babies."

She shrugged her shoulders. "I guess because they aren't selling to English speakers, so it doesn't matter."

The clerk at the check-out counter, like the handy girl, heard us speaking English and decided to show off her own language skills. "We have body bags on sale today!" she sad with a smile no-one had ever used to accompany a sentence with 'body bags' in it.

"Do they fit babies?" I asked, not expecting her to appreciate the double *entendre*.

Grocery Shopping: A Decide Your Own Fate Story

You are hungry. There is food in the house, but, unsurprisingly, you don't feel like eating tomato soup garnished with stale potato chips and cat food. You briefly consider skipping dinner and diving right into desert, but the only desert food you can find is vegan chocolate ice cream, which sounds about as appetizing as the cat food. Vegan strawberry sorbet would at least make sense, but vegan ice cream is a crime against any defensible culinary laws. The cream part requires milk and the milk part requires an animal with mammary glands. Without mammary glands, ice cream is just ice. Vegan chocolate can't make ice into a desert.

You have to go shopping.

As an American immigrant, it took you a while to understand grocery shopping in Germany, but this much you know: the supermarkets are divided into a few classes. At one end of the spectrum, there are stores that can be properly called supermarkets— they have fresh fruit and vegetables, delis, canned food sections, a bread aisle, and at least three different kinds of potato chips. Further, the supermarkets, while being considerably more expensive, have an important selling point: there is a very high chance that they have everything on a shopping list. So if you are desperate for a ham sandwich and aren't willing to settle for a chicken sandwich, it's best to pay the extra two euros and go to a supermarket.

At the other end there are what the locals call discounters. They have a meager selection of food which is priced so low the only way they stay in business is that enough people think it's a good idea to buy computers or lead-based paints at the same place they buy butter. In addition to the limited selection, when you visit a discounter close to closing time, there is a fair chance they won't have some of the more exotic items on your shopping list like bread or milk. Quite a few Germans don't seem to be bothered by this. As far as you can figure, they go to the discounter without a plan in mind and let whatever is in stock determine dinner. This perhaps explains why a lot of German food tastes like it was made from four ingredients.

The same complaint could be made about Mexican food, you think. The difference of course is that

Mexican food starts with ingredients that taste like something—peppers, tomatoes, corn, and spicy meat. So it's no surprise when the final result tastes like something. Since the Germans start with potatoes, flour, salt, and bacon fat, it's no surprise the final result tastes like leftovers.

As you make your way towards the stores, you think about what you want to have for dinner. A homemade pizza sounds good. A burger and a salad doesn't sound too bad either. It would also be a good idea to pick up a few essentials—bread, lunch meat, cheese, a bottle of wine—so there will be something for lunch tomorrow.

So, the only question that remains is where to go to buy these things.

If you would like to save money at the discounter, go to Section A (pg.97)

If you would like to spend a bit more at the supermarket, go to Section B (pg.101)

Section A

You arrive at the discounter at six o'clock, a good two hours before they are required by law to close. As you approach the store from its parking lot the first thing that strikes you is that the colors of the logo seem off somehow. Too many secondary colors.

In America, stores typically go for one of the primary colors—red or blue being the most common and when they add an accent color they go for yellow, another primary color. Primary colors look safe and powerful, so it's no surprise that these are also the colors of superheros—Superman, Spider-Man, Wonder Woman, Iron Man, Thor—all primary colors. The secondary colors are normally reserved for villains or minor characters. Green and purple for the Hulk, Green Goblin and the Riddler. Green, purple and orange for the Joker—the most powerful villain gets three secondary colors. For a grocery store, green could also be effective even though it's a secondary color. Green is an earthy color, the color of vegetables, so it fits. It works for Swamp Thing so it could also work for a grocery store. But purple and orange? Was the discounter trying to look villainous or were they just embracing their secondary status?

When you step inside, thoughts of superheroes and color theory leave your mind. Villainous lair or not, there's shopping to be done.

Just inside the doors is a gate. It only opens one way so after you step through, you are essentially trapped in the store. The only way out is to go through a cashier's line and in order to get to the cashier's line, you have to walk all the way to the back of the store and then double back on the other side of the inconveniently placed wall. The design, you are told, is to deter thieves, and the fact that it makes the customers feel like potential thieves instead of valued guests is irrelevant because all German grocery stores are designed this way, so it's not possible to vote with your euros and go to a supermarket built with a friendlier design philosophy. German grocery stores are the shopping equivalent of America's democracy —there are choices, but you feel dirty supporting either one.

On the other side of the gate, you find yourself in the produce section and start your hunt for dinner. You look around for a basket but then quickly remember that discounters don't have baskets. They do have shopping carts, but those are kept outside the store and are, because of the one-way gate, currently inaccessible. You see a few other customers piling groceries into box tops, and that seems like a good idea, but you don't see any empty box tops in the produce section. You decide to just hold on to whatever you find an hope that there will be an empty box along the way.

The produce section has lettuce, so the burger and salad plan has one ingredient in its favor. You also find some mushrooms so the homemade pizza plan could work as well. So far so good.

When you step into the bread aisle, things take a turn for the worse. Almost all of the bread is gone. There is a loaf of plain white bread—the Germans call it toast bread. You've had this kind of bread before and don't wish to repeat the experience so you keep looking.

Behind a package of cinnamon rolls you find a

package of full-grain bread. Unfortunately, it isn't American style full-grain bread, but the thinly sliced German variety that falls apart if you look at. It's completely useless for the burger plan. And aside from its structural problems, the taste is all wrong for a burger anyway. German-style full-grain bread has a deep earthy taste that, as far as you can tell, has been achieved by mixing the dough with earth, and perhaps bits of trees.

Since the burger plan has all but failed, you head back to the produce section and drop off the lettuce. That done, you head to the canned food section to check on tomato sauce for the homemade pizza plan. As luck would have it, they do have tomato sauce and just as you are about to grab a can, you think it would be a good idea to check on the other ingredients first. Cheese won't be a problem and some sort of meat should be easy enough to find, but pre-made pizza dough could be a challenge. Making pizza dough from raw ingredients is easy enough, but would easily add an hour to the production time, so that's out. You are way too hungry to cosplay as Jamie Oliver.

After some wandering, you find the section that should have pre-made pizza dough. The operative word though is 'should' because there isn't any there. There is pre-made croissant dough, sugar cookie dough, and gingerbread dough even though it's way past gingerbread season, but no pizza dough. There is a sign for pizza dough, but the space above the sign is empty. You briefly consider making a croissant pizza, but when you imagine what that buttery dough would taste like with salami, you put the package back on the shelf.

So, the pizza plan has failed as well. You are not sure what to do next. You could just leave empty-handed and go to the supermarket down the road, but that would mean you'd have to squeeze through the cashier's line without buying anything. The cashier is sure to give you a nasty look and you're not quite sure if you are up for that social interaction. The other option is to look around the store and find something else to buy so you don't have to go through the line empty handed.

If you would like to buy something else, go to Section C (pg.104)

If you would rather just squeeze through the line go to Section D (pg.105)

Section B

You arrive at the supermarket and are struck by its beauty, and a shopping cart. You apologize to the little old lady for not looking where she was going and step to the side.

To the left are the cashier lines. They are well-staffed for the dinnertime rush, so you don't worry too much about the line. Things would be different of course if this were a Saturday or a day before one of the thirty-five state holidays—the Germans always stock up on food the day before they are forbidden by law from shopping. Every Saturday in Germany reminds you of how the Americans emptied the store-shelves in the days leading up to the year 2000. Irrational or not, at the Americans thought the world was going to end. The Germans have no excuse for their behavior.

To the right is the bakery. You glance over and notice that there isn't much bread behind the counter and hope that the baguettes you can see in the oven will be on the shelf by the time you finish shopping. Baguette isn't needed for dinner, but would be nice for breakfast tomorrow.

Just past the bakery are the gates. Every German supermarket has them and you hate them. The gates only open one way and after you pass through them, the only way out of the store is to walk all the way to the back, circle around the other side of a wall, then go through a cashier's line. You've complained about these gate to your German friends before, but they didn't understand why they were so objectionable.

"They help the store protect their products from thieves," they said.

"Yeah, but," you replied, "it makes me feel like a potential thief instead of like a valued guest and potential customer."

They shook their heads. "You Americans and your customer service. There are more important things."

"Sure, but protecting cheap food at the cost of ruining a shopping experience isn't one of them."

"Ruining? Now you're just being dramatic," they said. And they were right—about the drama, not about the gates.

You pass through the gates and marvel at the fruit choices. The selection is impressive, albeit a tad pricey. You pick out a few good-looking apples and then realize you should get a shopping basket.

Just on your side of the one-way gates, you find the place where the shopping baskets should be. You look over towards the cashiers and see the baskets stacked up neatly waiting for an employee to bring them back around for the shoppers. If the gates weren't there, you could just grab one, but that kind of shopping experience is quite beyond your reach.

So, you could either walk all the way around the store and grab a basket from the back of a cashier's line and then walk all the way back to where you are now to get lettuce and veggies. Or, you could just use your backpack. Generally speaking, German stores don't like customers using backpacks for shopping. It's perfectly OK to bring in your own shopping bags— nearly everyone does that—but something about the straps of the backpack make the shop owners nervous.

If you would like to go around and get a basket, go to Section H (pg.111)

If you would like to use your backpack instead of a

basket, go to Section I (pg.113)

Section C

What the store doesn't have in food, they make up for with their selection of random household items. Running down the center of the store are large metal containers filled with a random assortment of things for the kitchen, the garage, the office, or a dungeon. It's actually a lot of fun to dig though them. You might find a set of screwdrivers, you might find a Jackie Chan movie for a euro, or you might find some fuzzy handcuffs with a matching cat 'o nail tails. Anything is possible at the discounter.

The first container you come to is filled with toys for toddlers, so you skip that one and walk over to the second container. You catch a glimpse of a plastic bag with what looks like a picture of Bettie Page on it and your interest is piqued. Maybe it's a costume and you can convince your friends to have a pin-up girl costume party, you think. But, upon further inspection, you see the package doesn't have a costume in it, but a seat cover for a car seat, and it's not exactly what you would call a tasteful car seat at that.

The third container has various electronic accessories: memory sticks, mousepads, compressed air, and tax declaration software. For a moment you consider trying to do your taxes by yourself this year, but then remember how frustrating it was the first time and put the software back. You grab an SD card and head for the checkout line.

As luck would have it, they open a new checkout line as soon as you make it back up front. You brush past a guy trying to move his cart into the newly-open line and pay for the SD card.

Once you are back outside you think about your next step. You could go to the supermarket—they will certainly have ingredients for both the burger and pizza plan. Or, you could just give up and go back home.

If you would like to admit defeat and go home, go to Section E (pg.107)

If you would like to go to the supermarket, go to Section B (pg.101)

Section D

As you make your way back to the front of the store you walk past the beer section. Even though you've decided to leave without buying anything, you briefly consider buying a six-pack just so you can avoid the awkward stare from the cashier, but when you look closer you see that the beer is in plastic bottles. You shake your head and steel yourself for the awkward stare. Even cowards have standards.

When you get to the cashier lines you notice that two of the five are open and have rather long lines. You think about going through an empty one and hopping the gate, but this thought is quickly quashed by the part of your brain that knows this would certainly invite a comment from a neighboring cashier. They might even tell you that that's not allowed and you'd have to go back and add shame to the embarrassment of squeezing past the waiting customers.

Decision made, you start to push your way past the waiting customers. At first the going is easy because the back of the line is still in an open area, but before long you are forced to slide between a customer on one side and the candy display on the other. You notice that they sell tiny bottles of schnapps alongside the candy and you wonder if any kid had ever asked a parent for one. An arm brushes against your leg and you mutter a few "excuse me's" and press on.

As you get to the cashier, you mistakenly make eye contact and she raises an eyebrow.

"Didn't find what you were looking for?" the cashier asks without even a hint of friendliness.

The less-than-polite question turns your embarrassment into derision. Why should you feel embarrassed because Germans can't design customer-friendly stores?

"No, I didn't. The beer is in plastic bottles and there's no way I'm eating sausage made out of blood."

The cashier scoffs and goes back to scanning items and you head outside.

As you step into the sunshine you think about your next move. You could just go home to the soup and stale chips, or you could brave the supermarket.

If you would like to admit defeat and go home, go to Section E (pg.107)

If you would like to go to the supermarket, go to Section B (pg.101)

Section E

On your way home, soup and stale chips sounds less appealing with every step, so you decide to swing by the gas station. It's only a block out of the way and they occasionally sell hot food, so it's worth a shot. Plus, unlike the discounter, the gas station will certainly have decent beer and it will be in glass bottles. The only downside to shopping at a German gas stations is that the prices are outrageous. What costs a euro in a supermarket will easily cost four in a gas station. They get away with these prices because German law requires grocery stores to close on Sundays but gas stations can remain open to sell groceries. You think it would be preferable the other way around: grocery stores should sell gas at four times the price and stay open all the time.

Once inside the gas station, you head back to the coolers to check out the beer selection. They have all of the local favorites and for the first time since leaving your apartment, you feel optimistic. You grab and overpriced six-pack and head around to the food counter.

There isn't much on offer: a few day-old doughnuts, some buns, a pretzel stick with some sort of cheese-goo baked into it, and some red sausages that actually look edible. The clerk sees you admiring, waddles over, and puts on a pair of plastic gloves.

"Hi." You smile. "I'll have one of those red sausages and one of those buns."

"No. Those are for currywurst."

"The buns or the sausages?" You hope it's the buns and there are other buns for the sausages that you can have. As far as you are concerned, curry is disgusting even when it's made by people named Nadeem Patel. When it's made by people named Hildegard Müller, it's a culinary crime on par with aerosol cheese.

"The sausages."

Four-letter words flash in your mind, but you compose yourself. As the Germans say, *die Hoffnung stirbt zuletzt.*[1] "I don't want currywurst," you say. "I just want a sausage with mustard. I'll pay for the extra bun."

"No, I can't do that."

"You *can* do that," you say slowly. "I'll pay for the currywurst and an extra bun. Just take one of those sausages, put it on a bun, and give it to me. Then I'll give you money. Actually, I'll take two."

1. Hope dies last.

"No. These sausages are for currywurst. Do you want currywurst?" You can see that she's losing patience with your unreasonable request.

"Can I get it without the curry sauce and an extra bun on the side?"

"No." She starts to take off your plastic gloves. "You need to go."

Your left eye starts to close involuntarily and you twist your head to relieve some of the tension in your neck. "OK. I'll just pay for this beer."

"I don't want any trouble. You need to go."

Saying nothing, you put the six-pack on the counter and walk out. When you get to the corner, you press the button for the pedestrian light and are pleasantly surprised when it turns green almost immediately. A few minutes later you are home.

There's still not much food in the house, but you do find a beer hiding under some very stale tortilla shells in the fridge. You open it and take a long pull.

Four pulls later the beer is empty and you feel a bit more composed. There's still enough time to go out again, but you're not sure if you are up to it.

If you would like to go back out, go to Section F (pg.110)

If you would like to just stay home, go to Section G (pg.111)

Section F

You grab your backpack and slam the door behind you as you head out to the street. As you start to walk, your legs protest. They, apparently, would much rather be propped up on the ottoman while the rest of your body gets numbed by a stiff drink, but they aren't in charge, so you trod on.

As you reach the corner, you realize that you haven't decided where to go. The obvious choice is to go to the supermarket. They will surely have the ingredients you need for dinner, but they are a bit further away, so you are not sure you can convince you legs to do it without whining.

The other option is to go back to the discounter. Sure, they didn't have what you wanted the first time you were there, but you could just lower your standards and buy some blood sausage, they always seemed to have lots of that in stock. Or, maybe they have restocked the shelves in the meantime. It's a possibility. After all, what kind of store would allow the shelves to remain empty during the busiest shopping times of the day? A German kind, for sure, but that particular one? Chance it?

As these thoughts bounce around your hunger-addled brain, another thought creeps in. What was that Einstein quote? Insanity is doing the same thing again hoping for different results? Was that it? Did Einstein really say that? Or was the quote apocryphal? Does it matter?

If you think Einstein was wrong and there's a chance things will turn out differently, go back to Section A (pg.97)

If you think that Einstein was right, go to Section B (pg.101)

Section G

Maybe it was the beer, but your desire to fight through a German supermarket has dwindled to nothing. You heat up a can of tomato soup, grab a bottle of bourbon from the cabinet and go to the living room.

Maybe after the soup, a drink, and some TV you'll feel like ordering a pizza, but for now the liquid dinner is all you have energy for. Besides, after a few drinks, the vegan chocolate ice cream might start to sound appealing.

THE END

Section H

You start to make the trip around the store to get a shopping basket. The trip would be faster if the aisles were a bit wider. For some reason the store insists on restocking the shelves during business hours, so some of the already narrow aisles are completely blocked by crates and boxes of goods waiting to be shelved. But you know that it's your own fault because you are the one who decided to go shopping hours before the store had to close . Basket in hand, you make your way back to the produce section to get some lettuce and mushrooms. Along the way you throw in a few essentials: room-temperature eggs, a box of milk—both of which used to seem strange but are now a normal part of the German shopping experience—some breakfast cereal, coffee, and hamburger buns.

Produce in hand, you make your way to the meat section and discover that there is no pre-package ground beef for the burger plan. But, this isn't a deal breaker. Unlike discounters, supermarkets have delis, and delis can always grind up more beef.

There isn't a line at the deli—Germans don't know how to form lines. It's occasionally possible to form a semblance of a line with Germans by forcing them between velvet ropes or walls, but the deli has neither of those things, so there's just a mass of people and shopping carts crowded around the glass meat-case.

You've seen this behavior before, of course. Whether it's getting onto a train, buying an ice cream from a street vendor, or escaping from a burning building, it's the same: the pushy get what they want—good seats, last waffle cone, air—and the pushovers get second-degree burns.

Burger isn't nearly as important as escaping from a burning building, so you aren't sure how to approach the situation. You could push your way to the front or be patient and hope that the person running the counter is keeping track of which customers are next in line.

If you feel like being pushy, go to Section J (pg.114)

If you feel like being patient, go to Section K (pg.115)

Section I

Just as you are about to throw a head of lettuce in your backpack, an employee interrupts you.

"Please don't use your backpack for shopping." There is no kindness in his voice.

"But there aren't any shopping baskets." You motion to the empty racks where the shopping baskets should be.

The employee puts down his pricing gun and gets close enough to make you uncomfortable. "We don't allow people to use backpacks here," he says, his unkind voice becoming an angry one.

Faced with an employee failing to be polite about the lack of baskets, you are confronted with a choice. You could either try to make your case more aggressively, or avoid any further confrontation and go get a basket.

If you feel like being aggressive, go to Section L (pg.116)

If you feel like avoiding confrontation, go to Section H (pg.111)

Section J

For a brief moment, you think about how best to approach the deli case without arousing the ire of the others who are waiting. One technique you've seen the Germans use is to pretend to check out the prices in order to get closer to the front of the group and then if the worker just happens to think you are next in line, then , well, it was the worker's mistake, wasn't it?

As you brush your way through the small crowd, you rub your eyes and squint at the price tags. You tap your jacket as if feeling for reading glasses and when you discover the pocket is empty, you squint again and move closer. When you get to the case, you suppress a smile—you are no lesser actor, after all.

When the worker asks who's next, you say nothing—that would be too obvious. The person next to you places an order and you bend down squinting at the price tags in the back of the case. You pull out your shopping list and are just starting to head back to your rightful place near the back of the crowd when the worker asks what she can get for you. Well, thinking you had any right to order was really her mistake, so you place an order for 300 grams of ground beef. For the first time in a while, you start to feel like you are integrating into German society.

Shopping is nearly over, go to Section M (pg.117)

Section K

You scan the crowd and make a mental note of those who arrived at the counter ahead of you. You know that the worker won't have done this, so it's up to you to make sure the deli is operating fairly.

As the crowd thins, you edge closer. A little old lady bushes past you, ostensibly to check the prices, and you prepare—you've seen this technique before. They pretend to check prices and when the worker turns to them, they'll have no qualms about taking your place in line, or in crowd, as the case may be. Well, not today, you tell yourself. After the man with the curly mustache, it's the sour-faced teenager's turn, and then it's your turn. The old lady will have to wait. Fixed income or not, fairness demands it.

"Who's next?"

The little old lady looks up and starts to raise an arthritic finger. "This man is next," you say slightly too loudly while indicating mustache-man, "and then the kid over there, and then me."

Everyone looks a bit surprised by your outburst, but the worker serves the people in the order you indicated.

The deli just needs some leadership, you think. Either that or a number system.

Shopping is nearly over, go to Section M (pg.117)

Section L

"Hey, there's no reason to get mad," you reply. "There are no baskets so I'm using this. It's no big deal." You try to keep your voice light, friendly.

"We don't allow that here."

"That lady over there is using a bag from home."

"That's not a backpack."

"Backpack or not, she's putting oranges into it. Why don't you go talk to her."

"I'm not worried about an old lady."

"You should be. They steal all the time."

"That not true."

"It is, actually, but that doesn't matter. I'll wait here. Why don't you go get me a basket?"

"It's not my job."

Now you know the conversation is over. You've heard this line before. When the lady at the watch counter refused to sell you a battery, it was because it wasn't her job. When the clerk in the clothing section refused to measure your sleeve-length, it was because it wasn't his job. And when the carpenters who installed your kitchen refused to sweep the floor before they left, well, that wasn't their job either, apparently.

You failed to negotiate the use of your backpack. Go to Section H (pg.111)

Section M

The grocery store has six cashier lanes and in order to accommodate the evening's final shopping rush three of those lanes are open. So, you only expect to wait fifteen minutes or so.

At the end of the lane there is a place to put your shopping basket—not at the end of the conveyor belt where it would make sense, but at the end of the lane. The conveyor belt is still a good ten feet away. So, what you have to do is wait until you are close to the belt, drop off your groceries, and then walk back through the line to drop off your shopping basket. When there is a line like there is today, this is an annoying process. Nobody ever offers to take the basket for you and half the time, the other people in line don't even make much of an effort to get out of your way—they just stand there chatting, holding bags of cat food, and silently judging you for having a basket instead of ten arms.

Today must be your lucky day, however, because no sooner do you turn around to bring your basket to the end of the lane does someone nod and offer to take the basket for you. You bow your head in thanks and for a moment are puzzled by his expression. He seems a bit surprised to have a basket in his hands and you think you might have misinterpreted his nod of offer as a nod of musical enjoyment—he does have headphones on, you notice.

The only admirable design feature of the German supermarket is the cashier's station. Unlike cashiers in the US, German workers are permitted to sit, which makes sense as there is no reason you can think of for a cashier to stand all day.

The cashier says hello and starts scanning your items and sliding them to the end of the station. There is no bagging service in Germany; the customers are responsible for bagging their own groceries. You notice that the cashier opens your egg carton, but you expected this; they do it every time. For years you thought they were just making sure that none of the eggs were broken, but that was American reasoning. You found out later that what they are really doing is making sure you aren't trying to steal a more expensive item by hiding it in an egg carton. You still aren't sure which expensive grocery store items would fit in an egg carton. Truffles? In any case, you wouldn't put anything into an egg carton anyway because EU regulations prevent eggs from being washed before being sold to customers. The thought is good: if farmers can't wash their eggs, there is more pressure on them to make sure their chickens live in clean conditions—good animal husbandry and all that. But the result is EU eggs are sometimes crusted with shit and on really special occasions chicken feathers are stuck in that shit as well. You don't think anyone would want to put expensive food items into a box with chicken feathers and shit, but maybe that's just you.

After bagging your groceries and paying, you walk over to the bakery counter. You don't really need anything, but it would be nice to have some baguette for breakfast. The line isn't any better organized here than it was at the deli, but there are only two people in front of you so things are almost easy enough for the employee to manage.

You don't see any baguettes when you get to the counter, but sometimes they have them tucked away. "Hi, do you have any baguette?"

"Oh, no," she replies, "we sold out of those a while ago. Would you like some Dosenbrot?"

"Dosenbrot?" You don't like the sound of that.

"Yeah, it's bread that's baked in a can so it has a harder crust than normal bread."

Normal German bread already has crust hard enough to scrape the skin off the roof of your mouth, so you politely decline.

On the way home, you stop by the neighborhood's beverage kiosk. The beer prices are only slightly higher than the prices in the supermarket, but unlike the supermarket beer, the kiosk beers are cold, so it's worth the extra few cents.

Once home, you throw the beer in the fridge and start making burgers. A short while later the smell of American-made burgers fills your German apartment, so you open the door. Like the Chinese family that lived under you when you lived in the US, you feel it is your duty to share the smells of home with your neighbors.

THE END

Barflies

Jim called me up and asked if I wanted to join him at the bar. After we both agreed that the Pope did indeed shit in the woods, I hopped in the shower to wash Sandra off of me. It was a Wednesday and married couples have their schedules.

Feeling fresh, I threw on a clean shirt, some dirty jeans, and my Chucks. After telling Sandra where I was going and giving her a kiss, I headed to the bar. It was just a few blocks away.

I found Jim in the back, looking out of place—much too young and too pretty to be in a dark bar intended for the older, local, less attractive population.

"Hey, Jim."

He looked up from his drink. "Oh, hey, Rob. That was fast. I haven't even finished my first one."

"Yeah, well, I wasn't doing anything. So here I am. What are we drinking?"

"I have to work tomorrow, so just beer for me. You might want to order something stronger."

I raised an eyebrow. "Why is that exactly?"

"Don't be mad. But Marcus is going to join us."

"Why would he be coming?"

"He read the first few chapters of my new book and wanted to give me some notes, so I agreed to meet him for a drink. I didn't want to hang out with him alone, so I called you."

"You conniving whore." I smiled. "You're lucky I like that Patrick Swayze ass you're sitting on."

"You're showing your age with that reference." He took a drink.

"Sorry, I don't know which young hot thing has the ideal ass these days."

"I don't either, to tell you the truth." He tilted his head. "Channing Tatum?"

"I don't know who that is," I said and then a guy I didn't recognize appeared at the table.

He pulled out a little notebook. "What can I bring you guys?"

"Where's Michael? It's Wednesday," I said.

"He's sick. I'm new."

I nodded. "Right on. I'll have a pilsner and a bourbon—a double Jim Beam if you have more in stock, otherwise Evan Williams is fine."

"I'm sorry, it's my first day. How big is a double?"

I was a bit confused by his question. "Twice as big as a single?"

"But that won't fit in a shot glass."

"Oh, you are new. I don't want a shot. I'm not a college student. Put it in a short tumbler. Two fingers or four centiliters or whatever measuring system you use here."

"OK. I can do that."

"Thanks, man." I smiled.

He looked at Jim. "Anything for you?"

"I'll have another weizen, but no lemon wedge this time."

The new guy nodded and wandered off. Jim finished his drink and looked up. "So, what's your problem with Marcus, anyway?"

"He's just so awkward, you know. He reminds me of those kids in high school that tried to impress the cheerleaders but just couldn't take the hint that they were embarrassing themselves."

"Are we the cheerleaders in that analogy?"

"I hope not. I look terrible in lollies."

Jim smirked. "Marcus isn't so bad."

"Did you know he's a premature ejaculator?" I said matter-of-factly.

"No." He chuckled. "How do you know that?"

"His wife is an old friend of Sandra's. She was over a few days ago and told us that he had used a desensitizing cream but didn't wear a condom, so naturally that cream got all up in Suzi. After a while she couldn't feel anything and freaked out. She thought she was having a stroke or something."

Jim giggled and shook his head. "That's too funny."

"I know, right? But it gets better. She kicked him off and then started rubbing and slapping, you know—trying to feel something, but it was too late. The cream had soaked in."

"Oh, my god."

"Yeah, she started crying and asked him to call an ambulance. He came clean—no pun intended—and told her about the cream."

He shook his head again. "That's too funny."

The new guy came back with our drinks. My bourbon was more of a double-double. "Wow, thanks, man, but you might want to make those a bit smaller before the boss gets mad. A single would be about this much." I showed him on the glass. "And a double about this much." I moved my finger up a bit.

"Do you want me to take it back?"

"Hell, no. I'll drink it, and I'll pay for two doubles if you want. I was going to order two anyway."

Jim and I paid attention to our drinks for a while and listened to the music. Elliott Smith. The new guy had better taste than Michael.

"There he is," Jim said.

I took a hit of the whiskey.

"Oh, hey guys." Marcus took a seat. "I didn't know you were coming out, Rob. Good to see you."

"You too, man." I raised my drink.

The new guy came back around and Marcus ordered a vodka sour.

"So, Marcus," Jim said, "what did you think of the first few chapters?"

"I liked them. I'm curious to see where it will go."

He and Jim talked about the book. I tuned out. Jim was good writer, but he wrote stuff I wasn't interested in—sea battles, adventures, people in armor traversing maps I didn't care about.

At some point, the new guy came back with the vodka sour.

"So, Rob, what are you working on these day?" Hearing Marcus say my name brought me back into the conversation.

"Oh, I decided to do something different. I'm writing a science fiction piece."

"That doesn't sound like you."

"Yeah, I need a break from the slice-of-life stuff. I want to broaden my audience. Young-adult science fiction seems like a good place to start."

Marcus nodded. "It can sell well. So, what's it about?"

"It's about an advanced civilization of flying insects who use their time machines to visit the arrow that Robin Hood used to kill the Sheriff of Nottingham. Sherwood forest becomes this vacation hot-spot for the creatures. Nobody in the forest notices, of course, because the creatures are pretty small. Fly on the wall and all that. It's a mix of sci-fi and historical fiction, but the over-all theme is how trends, no matter how ephemeral or trivial, can still inform a broader cultural context."

"Sounds interesting. Got a title yet?"

"Time Flies Like an Arrow."

Marcus's face darkened. "You're messing with me."

Jim started giggling.

"Wait until you hear about the antagonists that show up in book two. They're another advanced civilization of flying insects and they're all homosexual. They are quite fond of the banana that Ronald Reagan choked on. It's called—"

"OK, I get it—"

"Fruit Flies Like a Banana. It'll be more of a political piece about how Reagan-era policies damaged the homosexual community."

"Ha ha," Marcus said without laughing.

"What about you?" I said. "Up to anything interesting?"

"No, not really. Work keeps me busy. And things are a bit stressed with Suzi at the moment."

"Really?" I said. "She came over a few days ago and seemed happy enough."

"Yeah, I don't know. I think I need to spice up things in the bedroom." He looked at his drink. "I've been reading around. Have you heard of this cuckolding thing?"

"No," I said. "Well, I know about those birds that lay eggs in other nests, but—"

"No, not the bird thing. The idea is you invite some guy over to have sex with your partner and you just have to watch. It's like torture, but hot."

I put down my drink. "What is wrong with you?"

"What?" He got defensive. Maybe his drink hit him harder than he had expected and loosened his tongue a bit more than planned. "Do you mean that you wouldn't want to watch Sandra have sex with another man?"

"Of course not. That's disgusting. The idea of Sandra showing her O-face to another man is enraging. And if I had to watch it, I'd probably kill people. Starting with myself."

"Jeez, I had no idea you were so conservative."

"Just because I don't want to watch my wife getting railed by another guy, doesn't mean I'm conservative."

"So, you never wanted to spice up things in the bedroom?"

"Sure, who hasn't? But if you want to spice things up, buy some toys or some outfits. Do some role plays."

"I'm with Rob on this one," Jim interjected. "Especially the role play stuff. In the bedroom, I'm a teacher."

"Jim, you're a teacher in real life," I said.

"Yeah, but I can't have sex with my students."

"True. Anyway, Marcus, if you want to be sexually humiliated, just take off your pants and dance on our table. I'll laugh at you."

"Me, too," Jim said. "Anything for a friend."

"Thanks, guys. Not exactly what I'm looking for."

The new guy came back and we ordered another round.

"So," Marcus said, "neither of you would be interested in helping me out?"

"No way," Jim said. "Tuyet would kill me."

"Rob?"

"Not a chance. You don't want to see me naked anyway. I've got a bit of a dad bod."

"But you're so tall. I bet you could pick Suzi up and—"

"Could you stop thinking about me naked, please?"

The drinks arrived and I got the impression we were all glad for the interruption. A new song came on. The Pixies. I was starting to really like the new guy.

The conversation turned towards work. Marcus complained about how annoying it was to write a proposal for funding. Jim told a story about an international student who didn't know how informal rap lyrics were and had included quite a few colorful phrases in a formal essay. I listened and worked my way through the rest of my bourbon and beer.

The ice clinked in his vodka sour and Marcus got up. "All right, guys, I have to get going."

"Have a good night," Jim said.

I nodded. "See you at work."

He smiled, then went up to the bar to pay the new guy.

"That guy's got problems," Jim said.

"Seriously."

"You want another round?"

"Nah, I'm good. I think I'll head out, too."

Jim nodded and fished his wallet out. We paid and headed outside.

"All right, man," I said. "Until next time."

"Until next time."

When I got home, I brushed my teeth, got undressed in the living room so I wouldn't wake up Sandra, and then went into the bedroom.

When I got into bed, Sandra rolled over and threw her arm over me.

"Are you still awake?" I asked, barely above a whisper in case it was an automatic sleep-hug.

"Yeah. I finished the book I was reading just as you came in."

"Do you want to have sex with another guy while I watch?"

"What? No. That's messed up."

"That's good to hear."

"Why would you ask that?"

"The guys at the bar were talking about it."

"Are you drunk?"

"A bit. It's Wednesday."

A Zombie Cheerleader
Taught My Daughter English

If you want to make a good horror film, you have to be willing to torture the audience. You have to want to make the audience squirm, cry out in fear, and maybe wet themselves.

You have to be a sadist.

Without a little sadism, the horror film turns out to be unsatisfying: the scares are telegraphed, the camera cuts away from the action too soon, the antagonist comes across as weak or, worse, manageable. Good horror film directors know this and because they are willing to torture the audience, they turn out works of inspired madness that scare viewers for generations.

When my daughter was born, I often thought about horror films. Maybe it was the fact she had burst through a stomach rather than exiting in the normal way, maybe it was because she fed by sucking fluids directly out of Sandra's body, or maybe it was the projectile vomiting but, whatever the reason, the parallels were at the forefront of my mind. And when she became old enough to talk to, I often thought about the art of making horror films. I wanted her to turn out to be a decent person, so I had to be willing to be just a little bit sadistic.

Well, perhaps 'sadistic' is the wrong word. The Germans would say 'konsequent,' but I've never found an English word that quite captures what that word means. The basic idea is that a parent has to set rules and enforce those rules even if the kids balk, cry, or try to weasel out of compliance. This strategy leads to some squirming, some crying, and, sometimes, even some wetting.

Kids are lazy and, almost paradoxically, they will work very hard to be lazy. This laziness must be fought. Being *konsequent* was my chosen method. And, maybe, it was a kind of sadism. But, like the horror film director, it was a sadism that came from a place of love. If I had given in to all of my daughter's desires, if I had never pushed her to try harder, if I had never set rules or boundaries, she would have turned out to be the monster rather than the person who could handle them.

Our first major challenge was a linguistic one: she refused to speak English. By the time she could string German sentences together, my German was good enough to understand them, but I wanted her to learn my native language so she could communicate with the American side of our family. This alone was important enough to be *konsequent* on the matter. By the time she was two, she understood English just fine, but was too lazy to use it. She always tried to start conversations or answer my questions in German. I would feign ignorance.

"Daddy, ich hab' durst," she would say.

"What?" I'd reply even though I understood what she had said.

"Durst."

"What's that?"

She would make a drinking motion.

"Oh, are you thirsty?"

"Ja."

"What?"

"Yes," she would force out with an annoyed face.

"So, what do you want to drink?"

"Apfelschorle."

"What's that."

"Apfelschorle."

"Yeah, I heard you the first time. What is it?"

"Juice."

"Is it apple juice? 'Apfel' sounds like 'apple,'" I would say in a vain attempt to get her to realize that German and English weren't so different.

"Ja."

"What?"

"Yes."

"OK. I can get you some apple juice."

For months we spoke this way. She hated it. She hated English. I hoped she didn't hate me as well.

***

Part of the deal Sandra and I had worked out when I moved to German to get this Adams Family started was that I would be the principle caregiver so she could concentrate on her career. It was a good deal. She had to work, and I had to make lunch and play with toys. I still had my own classes to teach, of course, but I had moved all of mine to the mornings so I could be with Emma in the afternoons after daycare and in the evenings when Sandra had to entertain visiting philosophers. Emma and I would occasionally go to some of Sandra's work functions if they happened at child-friendly times, but we often found ourselves at home alone in the evenings, watching cartoons or playing with toys. During the busiest times of the semester, Sandra did a pretty good impression of the Invisible Man.

When a philosopher from Australia visited the department, Sandra and the other philosophers took him out to dinner after one of his talks. The dinner was early enough in the evening, so I tagged along with Emma in tow. The plan was to join the philosophers for dinner and then take Emma home to put her to bed, leaving the philosophers to their post-dinner bacchanalian ways. Or, if things went my way,

Sandra would take Emma home and I could engage in a little Bacchus worship.

Partway through the dinner the Australian heard me speaking English to Emma. "Oh, you speak English, too," he said to her.

"No, but my dad does," she answered.

He laughed. "But that was English, and you just spoke it."

She didn't respond. She had the look kids sometimes get when they are caught in a lie. But that's the same look they get when they don't understand philosophical humor, so it could have been that.

I understood Emma's lack of desire to speak English. None of her friends spoke English, nobody in public spoke English, it was just me and the random visiting professors. English was essentially dad's language. And learning a language to talk to one person was hardly worth the effort, especially if that person was nothing more than a parent.

After dinner and a few drinks, Sandra decided she wanted to hang out with her colleagues, so I packed Emma up and took her home. I stopped at the gas station on the way to get a bottle of wine. Once Emma was in bed, I could have my own philosopher's party.

Emma was happy that her vampire pajamas were clean, so getting ready for bed wasn't much of a struggle—until it came time to brush her teeth. Her little lips stretched closed as if they had been sewn together by a Cenobite, and there was no way to get the toothbrush in there without losing all of the toothpaste in the process. "Come on, honey, you need to brush your teeth."

She shook her head, lips firmly together.

"What does a werewolf do?"

She bared her teeth an growled. I took advantage and smeared her fangs with minty toothpaste.

Goodnight story finished and Emma happily snoozing with her plush bats, I settled down with a glass of wine to do some reading of my own on raising bilingual children. The book confirmed my experience: the language of the parents counts a lot less than the language of the child's peers. Since she didn't have any English-speaking peers in Germany, we had a problem. But as any good American knows, there isn't a problem that TV can't solve. So, the following morning, I introduced a new house rule: all TV shows that were made in the States (which was most of them) could only be watched in the original English. Dubs were henceforth verboten.

My hope was that she would recognize that English wasn't just that language her boring dad spoke, but it was also the language of the Sesame Street gang, Spongebob, and every superhero that anyone cared about. I wasn't sure why Germany never produced any superheroes, it seemed to be some sort of cultural deficiency. Perhaps it was because Hauptman Deutschland wouldn't have quite the same ring as Captain America. Although, on the other hand, I'd have been willing to read a comic staring Herr Doktor Tintenfisch, but, unfortunately, he didn't exist—not that Doctor Octopus really exists either, mind, but that's more of a philosophical point.

Emma loved TV time. Everyday after daycare we would sit down together and watch Dinosaur Train, Pee Wee's Playhouse, or Sesame Street—Gorden was her favorite because he once save Big Bird from some kidnappers. It was clear she understood the shows, but when she talked about them, she translated. While it was impressive that such a little thing could translate shows without thinking about it, it wasn't what I was going for.

****

After the university semester was over and Sandra and I had turned in our grades, we booked a flight to the States to visit my family. Emma had been there before as a baby, but this would be the first time where she would have to interact with people who didn't speak German. I hoped for the best.

The morning after our arrival, Emma walked up to her cousins, clearly excited to play with new kids and, perhaps just as importantly, their new toys. "Oh, die sind so hübsch. Darf ich mitspielen?"

"Baby girl," I said, "those girls don't speak German. If you want to play with their dolls, you have to ask in English."

She turned back to her cousins. "Your dolls are pretty. Can I play, too?"

I couldn't help but smile. Two complete sentences in a row. That was worth three round-trip tickets to Detroit already. The beaches, bagels, Budweiser, and burritos were just extra perks at that point.

Over the next few weeks, Emma's English improved dramatically. I had expected it was there just needing a kick. Wanting to play with kids was that kick. And when we returned to Germany a few weeks later, I was pleased to see that Emma didn't revert back to German with me. The switch had been flipped, and our forced conversations were over. She still needed some practice with pronunciation and some help with some grammar, but I was sure I could help with that. I was an English teacher, after all.

When fall rolled around, the clouds rolled in, and Emma and I were stuck inside. After a week, I was sick of Emma's toys, so I put her in some rain gear and walked her downtown. We needed new toys to play with.

The closest toy store to us was the Lego store, so we ducked in, shook off the rain, and wandered around. I wanted everything—the ninjas, the knights, the superheroes, even the fairies. Unfortunately, I didn't have eighty-thousand euros in my pocket.

I felt a tap on my arm and turned around. It was a former student of mine.

"Hey, what's up, Ralf?" I said. "I didn't know you

worked here."

"Yeah, I just started a few weeks ago. Are you looking for anything special?"

"No. Just wanted some new toys to play with since it's too wet to go to the park."

"Do you like Halloween?"

"Of course. I'm an American."

"We just got some Halloween figures in stock. Do you want to see them? We have them in the back office."

"For sure." I turned to Emma. "Come on, baby girl, let's go look at some of the new ones."

Ralf led us to the back office and showed us the Halloween minifigures collection. Witches, the Wolfman, a mad scientist—all of the classics from a childhood spent watching old movies with my mom. I wanted them all for Emma's childhood.

"Can I buy these?" I asked.

"No. We're not allowed to yet. But you can have a few if you want."

"Really? Your boss won't mind?"

"No, it's OK. We're allowed to give away a few minifigures to friends."

Emma and I picked through the figures. She decided on the zombie cheerleader, and I went with a fly monster—it was based on the classic 50s Fly, not the Jeff Goldblum 80s Fly.

Before we left, I bought a little Scooby Doo set as a thanks to Ralf for hooking us up and then we headed back out into the rain. When I opened our umbrella, an idea hit me.

"You know what we should do?" I asked. "We should make a movie with our new toys."

"How do we make a movie?"

"We just have to take a bunch of pictures and stick them all together on the computer. It will look like they toys are moving."

"Can I be the cheerleader?" she asked.

"Sure. I'll be the fly. But first we have to think of a story and then build some sets out of the Legos we have at home."

"What's a set?"

"Like little houses or whatever. Places where the story happens."

We started to think of ideas for our movie and by the time we got home, we had a basic plot. The Fly and Zombie Cheerleader were the bad guys. They would capture a professional wrestler, and his young friends would stage a rescue. A classic tale of friendship, adventure, monsters, and mullets. Tobe Hooper would have been proud.

Over the next few rainy weeks, we built the main set-pieces of our film: a path through a forest leading to a castle, a spooky hallway, and a throne room for the big finale. After everything was built, Emma and I moved the pieces by millimeters and took pictures. When she got bored, I'd let her watch a show while I continued. When she went to bed, I would pour a glass of wine and continue.

After the animation was complete, we started to record the voices. Since we had done the animation before the voices, we had to write lines that fit with the film instead of recording lines and then animating to fit the audio. That would have been smarter, but we didn't really know what we were doing.

Recording the voices was my main motivation for making the film as it gave me an excuse to work on Emma's pronunciation. She would say her line, I'd coach her through the difficult sounds, she'd repeat it until it sounded natural. Had this been a classroom situation, she would have gotten bored. But since it was a zombie-cheerleader situation, it was easy to maintain her interest.

After a few days, we finished the main voice track, which included one of the better cheers in recent memory: One, two, three, four. I'm gonna eat you on the floor.

"OK, baby girl. We've got the voices, now we need some sound effects," I said one afternoon after daycare.

"What are sound effects?"

"You know, like the sound of breaking glass and people screaming. Stuff like that."

"Can we break a glass?" she asked.

"No. I'll look on the internet for that one. We don't want mommy to get mad."

"I can scream." She took a deep breath.

"Aieeeeeee!"

"Not bad. Not bad." I nodded and rubbed my chin like Herbert West surveying his reanimated work. "But how about we scare some of your friends and record them screaming? What do you think about that?"

She narrowed her eyes. "Is that mean?"

"No, of course not." I said. "Little kids scream all the time. Get your zombie mask and let's go to the park."

And so we went. Emma chased the kids, and I recorded the chaos. Our film would have that touch of realism necessary to separate it from other films in the Lego Zombie Cheerleader genre. And I only had to explain to one parent that we were Americans celebrating Halloween.

While Emma was in daycare the next day, I compiled a list of music that we might want to use. After picking her up and returning home, I sat her on my lap and played her the options.

"How about this one?" I asked.

"Oh, I like this. It's fun." She bobbed her head from side to side.

"Then not that one." I hit the stop button and started the next piece. "How about this one?"

"I don't like it. It's scary."

"Then that's the one we should use. We're making a scary movie, remember?"

We listened to a few other pieces to fit different

parts of the movie and then it was time to go grocery shopping, make dinner, and do all of those other things that families without film projects do. But after Emma went to bed, I added the music to the film. All we needed was a title.

The next morning at breakfast, we brainstormed.

"What should we call our movie?" I asked.

"I don't know. We could call it *The Fly*. He's the bad guy."

"Good title, but there's already a movie called that. Two, actually. You can watch them when you're older."

"What do you think?" she asked with a mouth full of Count Chocula cereal.

"I don't know." I shrugged my shoulders. "How about *Zombie Cheerleaders Kidnapped My Friend*?"

"I don't like it."

"Yeah, it's not very good." I took a sip of my coffee. "What's the wrestler's name?"

"I just call him Too Much. My cousins said that."

"What?" I giggled. "They said he's *too much*?"

"Yeah, that's what they said."

"Then let's call the movie *The Fly Who Knew Too Much*."

"OK," she agreed, but I was sure she didn't get the joke. She was old enough for Lego zombie cheerleaders, but not nearly old enough for Alfred Hitchcock.

After I dropped Emma off at daycare, I finished the title card and credits. The movie was finished.

I uploaded it to the internet and sent the link to my brother. My thinking was that he could organize a movie night for his girls and set up a video conference call with us so Emma could see how her cousins reacted to all of our hard work.

The following weekend he did just that. When the call came in, I put Emma on my lap and we watched the American side of the family watch our movie.

They loved it. The cousins couldn't stop giggling and Emma couldn't stop smiling. I gave her a squeeze and kissed the back of her head. But when the zombie cheerleader showed up, the littlest cousin started to squirm and then ran out of the room.

"Hey, dad, I think Heather wet herself." She giggled.

"I think you're right. Is our movie too scary? Were we mean?"

She turned around to face me, and for a moment I was happy she didn't have platinum-blonde hair and glowing eyes. "No. Little kids wet themselves all the time." A sadistic smirk spread across her little face. "It's a scary movie, remember?"

Lecture Notes on The Metric System

Since I was never into hard drugs when I lived in America, I had very little experience with the metric system. I had seen kilos in the movies, but had never hefted them for weight. Lines I had seen in real life, but as far as I know, a line is not a practical unit of measurement.

The problem is, neither are grams. When I moved to Europe, I was forced to use this drug-movie system and quickly discovered that estimating the weight of things in grams is impossible. In 1795, the French government defined a gram as "the absolute weight of a volume of pure water equal to the cube of the hundredth part of a meter, and at the temperature of melting ice." Now hold that image in your head and try to make a cake.

The American system of weights operates under a much   different   assumption: We   base   our measurements on things people already have in their kitchens: cups, tablespoons, a pinch. Unlike the hypothetical perfect cube of nearly freezing water, a cup is defined as "the amount of stuff that will fit in a cup." You want a big cake? Use big cups.

To make matters worse, the metric system wasn't just for the kitchen, where I had scales; it followed me into the city. The question I got most often from the Lilliputian denizens of Germany was: "My God, how tall are you?" With no meter stick available, I would extend my arms thinking that seeing my height lengthwise, like da Vinci's Vitruvian Man, might help. (It didn't.) When they asked how tall my wife was, I took a different tack: "Her nipples chafe on my belt."

I could have estimated in feet, of course, that would have been easy. A foot is about the size of, not surprisingly, a foot. You want to know how wide a room is? Walk across the room. Heel to toe. And count. You want to guess how tall someone is? Just imagine how many times you would have to step on them to get out of a burning building. It's not hard. I'd guess my wife is a bit more than five feet tall. So, not tall enough to slow down my escape.

Centimeters are a different story. They are really small — about the size of a fingertip. So if I want to guess how tall someone is, I have to imagine how many times I'd have to poke them, which is impossible unless you are some sort of super-specific idiot-savant. I could probably guess how tall a smurf is using the "what-if-I-poked" method, but humans are too big and centimeters are useless to me.

But, as much as I dislike centimeters and grams, I don't hate them.

I hate Celsius.

I don't hate it because I think it's unreasonable. I hate it because whenever it comes up in conversation, some smug European rushes to defend its honor, as if Thermometer Lives Matter. "Celsius is so much more elegant, more civilized," they say with a haughty air. "Water freezes at zero and boils at a hundred." And then they smile as if they came up with it. As if that's what's wrong with America.

Look, why would I care about when water freezes? I don't live in the water. I'm not a fish. I live in the air with the rest of civilization. And for the air, Fahrenheit is a much more useful system. In Fahrenheit, zero is really very cold — you walk to school, the snot crystallizes inside your nose and you hate life. That's zero. One hundred is really very hot — you hug your tiny wife, she sticks, and says sex will have to wait until the air conditioner kicks in. That's a hundred. And fifty is a perfect spring day for golfing.

In Celsius, on the other hand, zero is only kind of cold. Maybe wear a hat? At one-hundred all of the Earth's oceans are gone and life as we know it has ended. And at fifty, the slaves building the FIFA soccer stadiums in Qatar start to die. So, I really don't want to hear about elegant, civilized systems from

Europeans.

But they aren't changing, and I'm not moving, so I guess I'll have to make my peace with it. It won't be easy, but a journey of a thousand miles starts with a single step. Just don't tell me how long that is in centimeters.

Paternalism

aving a baby in Germany is a bureaucratic nightmare. Things are even worse if the parents aren't married. And the first time around, we weren't. After the 26-hour labor, the real work began, which is to say I had to visit a great number of offices to procure a greater number of documents. And the first document we needed granted the baby a name.

The baby's first name had to be on a state-approved list. This, I was told, was to protect the baby from having a name which might one day cause it harm. But since the names 'Gluthilda' and 'Günther' *were* on the list, I didn't exactly know what they meant by 'harm.'

If it were just a matter of finding a name on the list, things might have been easy enough, but for us there was a further problem: we wanted a name that was more-or-less normal in both English-speaking and

German-speaking circles. And while traditional American names were on the list, many American names were strongly associated with Germany's lower classes. Since we didn't want our future son's future teacher to assume he was a fifth-generation undesirable who would never amount to anything other than a domestic abuser, we had decided he couldn't be Kevin. We were relieved to learn that the baby didn't have a penis, which meant the Kevin problem was entirely avoidable.

The last name is, obviously, easier, but not without difficulties for unmarried parents. If the parents aren't married, the baby's last name is automatically the same as the mother's, and if the parents want to change it to the father's name, there is a form and a fee. The mother must agree to this change.

After the name is approved, there is the matter of parental rights to attend to. Initially, the unmarried father has nearly no rights to the baby at all. If the parents wish the father to have rights to the child, there are a few forms to fill out. One form requires the father to pay child support if the parents stop living together, but doesn't, as far as I remember, grant any decision-making rights nor any visitation rights. If the parents want those, there is an additional form. And as with the baby's last name, the mother must agree to grant the father these rights. If she doesn't, the father must take the mother to court. I'm not sure how well a foreign father would fare in a German court against a German mother. I would assume it's fair enough, and I'm also glad I never had to test this assumption.

I should say, however, in the interest of fairness, that some of these laws have since been changed to make life a bit easier for unmarried fathers here in Germany, but we had to deal with this way back in the misandric days of 2007.

A few years after the first baby and a few days after procuring the last document, the second baby was on its way. Going through all of the paperwork required for non-married couples a second time weighed heavily on my mind and inspired me to action. I got down on one knee, picked up a beer cap I had dropped, and went to find Sandra.

"We should get married before this one comes," I said. "It would be less work."

She looked up for her book and shrugged her shoulders. "Sure."

And some people say romance is dead.

The first step towards matrimonial bliss was to schedule an appointment with a clerk at the Rathaus, which is the German word for City Hall but literally translates to 'Council House.' This is easy to remember because it's natural to imagine rats forming councils. We decided to schedule our meeting on a Thursday since that was the only day the offices were open to the public later than 1:00. Once there, the clerk, a bald man with eyebrows so blond they were nearly invisible, walked us through the list of documents we would need to obtain before we could get married. And what a list it was.

Some of the documents were predictable enough: state-issued photo IDs, birth certificates, and so on. Some of them required stamps and seals I had never heard of; I had never heard of an Apostille Stamp, for example. One of the documents could only be given in person, which would have required me to go to the US Embassy in Frankfurt. But some of them were downright weird, like a document that stated I wasn't currently married in my home state.

"Excuse me," I said. "Can you explain document number five?"

"Yes, we need a document issued by your home state that states that you are not currently married."

"OK. I'm not sure that document exists in the USA, but assuming it does, which state is my home state? Ohio, where I was born; Michigan, where my parents live and where I went to high school and university; or Missouri, where I most recently lived and worked?"

His eyes bulged a bit more, clearly not understanding why I couldn't understand something so simple. "We need a document issued by your home state that states that you are not currently married." He shook his head slightly and when his jowls jiggled I couldn't help but to wish he had eyebrows. Without them, his bulging eyes and loose skin made him look like someone had glued googly-eyes to a discarded foreskin.

"That helps a lot, thanks."

I considered telling him that the USA was in fact one country and not fifty, so, as a citizen of that country, I could have easily gotten married in any one of the fifty states, but really, what would have been the point?

To complicate matters, all of my documents (even the ones that didn't exist in the US) couldn't be more than six months old and needed to be translated and stamped by a state-licensed translator. These translations could also not be more than six months old.

It wasn't that they wanted the information that irked me, that much I understood, it was that they didn't trust me to simply give them the information. I knew when and where I was born, so why couldn't I just write that down?

When we got home, I threw the document list in the trash.

Annoyed but unperturbed, I hopped on the internet. There had to be an easier way. And after a few clicks, I saw that there was. According to the County Clerk's Office website of Muskegon, Michigan, all one needed to get married there was a photo ID, 11 dollars, and a willing partner who also had a photo ID and 11 dollars. But I had been living in Germany too long and couldn't believe it was that simple, so I rang them up.

"County Clerk's Office. How can I help you?" a light and friendly female voice answered.

"Hi, I'll be in Michigan around Christmas and would like to get married. What do I need to bring with me?"

"You need a photo ID with a birth-date on it. The license costs 22 dollars."

"OK, but my fiancée is German, not American. What does she need?"

"She needs a photo ID with her birth-date on it." There was some confusion in her voice as if she thought answering the same question twice was strange.

"That's it?"

"Yeah, that's it. We just need to make sure you are both over 18."

"Do we need to make an appointment?"

"No, it's not necessary. We're open Monday through Friday from 8:00 to 4:45, but it takes a little while to fill out the forms, so you should try to come before 4:00."

I thanked her and hung up.

A few weeks later, we were there in person and told the clerk (I wasn't sure if it was the same clerk from the phone call) we wanted to get married.

"OK," she said. "Do you both have IDs with you?"

"Yes, we do," I said.

"Good. So, fill out these forms. There's one for each

of you. But, do not sign them. Once the forms are filled out, bring them back to me."

The forms were relatively straightforward: name, current address, birth-date, birth-place, parents' names, date of previous marriage and divorce, etc. Basically, everything the people in Germany wanted to know for a wedding there but without all of the supporting documentation and official stamps which proved the information was accurate.

After filling out the forms, we returned to the clerk.

"OK," she said, "raise your right hands."

We did.

"Is everything you wrote here true?"

"Yes, everything is true," we said more-or-less together.

"OK. Now, you can sign."

And that was that. I had almost forgotten how it felt to be treated like an adult.

We had to wait three days for the forms to be processed and the license to be printed. After we picked up the marriage license, we walked across the street to the court house.

About the only negative part of our marriage experience was entering that court house. Like most every other public place in Muskegon, Michigan the court house was run-down and filled with people who inspired misanthropy in others. Why people getting married and people standing trial for murder need to share the same place was and is still beyond me, and the security guards didn't know why people are entering the building, so they treated everyone with the same humorless contempt.

"Please remove all metal objects and place them in a tray, then step through the metal detector," one of the guards said as we approached.

"Sure thing," I said. "Do I have to remove this boutineer? It has a small metal pin in it."

"If it will be detected by the metal detector, then remove it."

Not being an expert on metal detectors, I found the answer lacking. "But I don't know how sensitive this machine is, which is why I asked." I wasn't trying to be difficult, I just really hated putting those things on. I could never get them to stick on right. And considering the fight I had had with the one currently pinned to my jacket, I was lucky the flower had any pedals left to worry about.

"If it will be detected by the metal detector, then remove it."

I wasn't sure if he hadn't heard me and was just repeating the same line to the next person or had heard me and was just being an asshole. Not wanting to test the latter theory, I removed the boutineer.

As I was walking away, I heard him talking to the other guard about how the detector was so sensitive it had once been set off by a scratch-off lottery ticket, and the asshole-theory was confirmed.

Paternalism

After a quick stop by the front desk to find out where we needed to go, we made our way to the court room. The magistrate was waiting for us. I guess if you work in a court house in an economically depressed area, marrying people is probably one of the best parts of the job, so why be late? He was a friendly-looking man in a chocolate suit who seemed genuinely happy to see us. He smiled so broadly that for a moment I thought I knew him, or should have known him—Had we gone to school together? Had I dated his sister?—But then I remembered that that's just the way Americans smile, so I smiled back. Broadly. I was home.

After handshakes and a few pleasant words of instruction, the ceremony began. A few minutes later, I was kissing my wife in front of a stranger—and then Emma broke free of my mother's grasp and ran up to us.

She was not a happy little girl. She didn't exactly know what a wedding was, but from what she had gathered listening to the ceremony, it had something to do with being a family. She insisted that she be married to us too since she was a part of the family and shouldn't be left out, but after giving her some kisses in front of the magistrate, she felt better.

A few months later and back in Germany, we received the official copy of the marriage license in the mail. We translated it, paid someone we found on the internet 15 euros to stamp the translation—which proved that the translation had been done by a state-approved and licensed translating expert rather than people who merely spoke the languages—returned to the Rathaus to file the license, and were then considered to be officially married in Germany.

I still don't know what an Apostille Stamp is.

Naked German Children

The schoolyard was wall-to-wall naked children and nobody seemed to care. I didn't care either, I just wished a few more of them were darker. I could appreciate Germany's stance on naked children: children are not sexual beings, so being clothed or unclothed is inconsequential. I just wished Germany would appreciate my view on integration: finding your blond-haired, blued-eyed boy on the school playground is easier if there are a few naked brown kids running around.

I tried hard not to look surprised, but I hadn't seen so many naked kids in one place before. And the nudity was only part of the culture shock, the other part had to do with the penises—anteaters every one, not a mushroom in the bunch. They made me think of the conversation I'd had with Sandra after the first time we had sex. She was a German exchange student and had her own culture shock when she found herself in bed with an American.

"So, you're circumcised?"

"Yeah, most Americans my age are, I think." I leaned back on the bed and put my hands behind my head.

"But there's so much less to play with."

I shot her a skeptical eye. "No one has ever said that about my penis before."

She blushed, thinking she had insulted me. She hadn't. It would have been hard to feel embarrassed by my penis while it was in the hand of a cute exchange student.

A little boy looked up at me. I hoped I hadn't been staring, lost in happy memories.

"What's your name?" he asked.

"Rob."

"What?"

"Rob."

"What?"

"Rob." Adult Germans always had a hard time understanding my name. It's only three letters but each letter is pronounced differently enough from the corresponding German letter that they got confused. The German 'r' is a guttural roll which sounds a bit like you are trying to clear your sinuses, the 'o', unlike the English 'o' is pronounced like the 'o' in 'rope,' and the 'b' has a light popping sound, like the first 'p' in 'pop.' So, my name, in the German mouth, sounds like Gollum trying sing bebop. Apparently, naked German children weren't any better at understanding it in an American accent.

"Rob?"

"Yeah, that's right." I was impressed with his pronunciation. Maybe kids were better at languages than adults.

"But 'Rob' isn't a name." So much for that theory.

"I'm pretty sure it is. Do you know where David is?"

"Yeah, he's over there playing with Hannes."

"Is 'Hannes' a name?" I asked as sarcastically as my German would allow.

"What?" It wasn't enough, apparently.

I found my boy splashing in a sprinkler with a few of his friends.

"Hey, baby, you ready to go home? Where are your clothes?"

"They're over there with Eliza's."

"That's my boy. Come on. Let's get dried off and say bye to your teacher."

We found his teacher helping a girl find her underwear. We said our goodbyes and headed out.

"Did you have fun at school today."

"Yeah, we played in the water."

"I saw that. Will your group do anything special on Friday? It's your last day. After the summer break, you'll go to the big kids school."

"I don't know. My teacher didn't say something."

"Anything."

Once home, we sat down to play some video games. We normally had about half an hour to ourselves before my daughter came home from school. So, he had first choice of TV activities, and that choice normally involved a Mario game.

"Hey, Dad, is Mario Japanese?"

"Yeah, why?"

"Then I know some Japanese words."

"Like what?"

"Mamma mia!"

"That's Italian, kiddo. Mario is a supposed to be an Italian plumber."

"So I know some Italian words then."

"Yep."

We played a few levels, but he wasn't very into it and took off to his room. I played a bit more and then noticed it was a bit too quiet in the apartment. When kids are loud, everything is fine, but when it gets quiet, it's best to see what they are up do.

I stuck my head in his room. He had taken off his pants and underwear, but it was hot and that part was understandable. The way he was playing with his rocking horse was less understandable.

"Baby boy, get your penis out of that horse's nose-hole." I didn't think it was a sexual act, and I wouldn't have cared even if it had been. More likely, it was just that kids like to see which things fit inside other things and boys have an obvious thing to do science with. Besides, if you can't feel comfortable masturbating with a rocking-horse at home, then it's not a home. But, all the same, I didn't want to deal with stuck parts.

Shaking my head and giggling, I couldn't help but think about a linguistics class I'd had as an undergraduate where we discussed communication systems. One feature human languages have that animal communication systems seem to lack is that humans are productive with language, which means they can use language to describe new situations. Potentially, there are an infinite number of sentences a speaker could utter, but I'd imagine there aren't very many that involve 'penis' and 'rocking-horse nostril.'

The door-bell rang. It was Emma. She came in with a friend from school, Lena, a shy girl who had somehow maintained her birth-weight throughout elementary school.

"Dad, can Lena stay for a while?"

"Sure, what do you girls want to do?"

"Can we watch TV?"

"Sure." Parenting made easy.

The girls made their way to the living room. Along the way, Lena glanced into my son's room. He was playing with some dinosaur toys and was still naked, at least where it counted.

"Why doesn't your brother have clothes on?" Lena

seemed a bit uncomfortable. She was only a few years older than David, but those few years made the difference it seemed, at least as far as comfortableness with exposed penises goes.

"I don't know," Emma answered. "What do you want to watch?"

I got the girls situated in front of the TV and then went out on the balcony to read the personal ads in my wife's news magazine. I wasn't looking for anyone, of course, but I needed to practice my German, and imagining what the writers of these ads were like was as good a way as any. It was clear they weren't tech savvy, modern people since they were posting in a magazine instead of on the internet like a normal person. Beyond that, most of them fell into predictable patterns.

There were the sugar-daddy seekers: Twenty-five-year-old woman seeks thirty-five to fifty-year-old man for travel, skiing, golf, fine dining, and spending time on boats.

There were the career women who learned that life in an office isn't terribly fulfilling: Thirty-eight-year-old professional woman looking to have children with the right man.

And the idiots: Sagittarius woman on the hunt for Mr. Right. Desire for a spiritual relationship, organic dinners, deep conversations, and homeopathic advocacy a must!

I didn't understand why they weren't honest. It

had only take me a few months to learn the code words Germans used to attract mates, so I was sure their target audience was already in the know, so what was the point? If everyone knows the code, there's no reason to write in code. They should have written something like, "I'm willing to sleep with you if you are rich and will buy me stuff," or "lonely sperm donor wanted," or "I'm scientifically illiterate and want to share my bubble with another person who believes in magic."

If things didn't work out with Sandra, maybe I would be desperate enough to write a personal ad—but on the internet, of course, like a normal person.

I heard the theme song of the kids' show and figured the girls had watched enough, so I went back to the living room to turn the TV off.

"Dad, can't we watch another episode?"

"No, that's enough. Why don't you go outside and play?"

"It's too hot to go outside. Can we have ice cream?"

"I don't think we have any left. You can have some ice *water.*"

"Come on, Lena, let's go to my room."

"So, no ice water?"

The girls headed to my daughter's room. I went to my son's room and offered to play with him under the condition that he put underwear on. He agreed and we built a gladiator arena out of blocks.

"Boom. Ha ha, dinosaur. I went to the Batman

store. Now you are not anymore alive." His English could have used some work, but I was intrigued by the Batman store.

My daughter's window must have been open, because I could hear the girls talking. They were giggling about something, but I couldn't quite make it out. From what I could tell, they were writing a note to someone. The giggles suggested a boy. The disagreements suggested they didn't know how to write notes to boys. I thought about sliding my wife's magazine under the door to give them some ideas, but then thought better of it. The code of elementary school kids was probably different.

After a few more battles, Sandra came home. She gave us all welcome-home kisses, complained a bit about the hot bus, and then we made a shopping list. I offered to make the trip to the store. After a hard afternoon of playing video games, reading personal ads, and kicking Batman's ass, I needed a break.

I put on some headphones, queued up Maceo Parker's *Life on Planet Groove*, and headed out. By the time Maceo started his solo, I was at the check-out line. The second the fist song was over, I stepped into my apartment. One of my great joys was when the soundtrack provided by my headphones matched the world outside.

"I'm back," I said, taking off my headphones.

"I'm in the kitchen," Sandra said.

I kicked off my shoes and went into the kitchen.

"Where are the kids?"

"In their rooms playing."

"Is Lena staying for dinner?"

"No, she had to go home."

"Right on. So, I couldn't find those eyeglass cleaning tissues, but I got everything else."

"You could've asked someone where they were."

"They were all busy working."

She rolled her eyes a bit. She knew I didn't like talking to people I didn't know.

"I did remember to get myself some shower gel."

"I bought some yesterday."

"You bought you shower gel, but I don't want to smell like flowers and fruit. I'm still a man even if I do have a sewing machine. I want to smell like leather and maybe tobacco. I want to smell like I punched a bear."

"That doesn't have a smell."

"Yes, it does. A man smell."

"I like the way you smell without soap."

"I know you do. I still remember when you asked me to send you one of my shirts when we were doing the long-distance relationship-thing. I wore that thing for three days before I sent it to you."

"That's right. I forgot about that. I liked that smelly shirt. It help me sleep."

"See. Man-smell. It's narcotic."

She shook her head, but I could tell she agreed. I finished putting away the groceries we didn't need for dinner, and started to chop onions. "You missed a good show at the pre-school today," I said. "There were lots of naked kids running around."

"They're lucky. It's too hot for clothes. Adults should be able to walk around naked, too."

"I'm going to have to disagree with you there."

"You Americans are so prude."

"I'm not prude. I have to use the bus."

"What's that have to do with anything?"

"Well, one nice thing about clothes is they soak up a bit of the sweat. I don't want to plop my naked ass down in a seat after some sweaty dude moistens it for me."

"Gross. Maybe that's why nudists carry towels."

"I didn't know they did. I don't know anything about nudists. I've seen a few videos on the internet, but they weren't exactly documentaries."

"Yeah, I know all about your internet videos. You should close the browser when you finish, by the way."

"It's my computer. If you want to use it to check your email, you take on certain risks."

She laughed and agreed that she had no right to complain.

"I think we're about set here. You wanna call the kids?" she asked.

I called the kids in, grabbed a beer for myself, and we all sat down at our little table.

"So, baby girl, how was school today?"

"Pretty good." She had a sly smile.

"More than good," Sandra added. "She sat with Jacob at lunch is what I heard."

"Damn, girl. Nice. You bagged the Jay." Jacob was the most sought-after boy in my daughter's class. Cute, athletic, and until recently, interested in my daughter's best friend, Karola. But Karola moved to Berlin a few months ago. Sometimes number two gets promoted.

After dinner, we went through the bedtime routine: brushing the kids' teeth, good-night stories, kisses. Once the kids were tucked, I opened another beer, and sat down on the sofa. Sandra came in.

"What are we doing tonight?" she asked.

"I've got no plans."

"We could get naked."

I tried to do the sexual performance equation as quickly as possible. I figured my default time was a more-than-adequate-for-Sandra twelve minutes. Every beer added five, but if the number got beyond thirty, I wouldn't be able to finish at all. Giving myself hand earlier in the day could easily add fifteen minutes, so it was risky to drink after a private session. On the other hand, every day without subtracted maybe three minutes from the default, so it was a good idea to have a long pull from the bottle when I was about to come off a dry spell. Of course, other things could affect the equation: a certain look, a certain quiver, a certain hair stuck in my mouth — external things beyond my control. But unlike Blaise

Pascal, I didn't include uncertainties in my decision matrices.

The math was in my favor, so I agreed.

When I woke up the next morning, the bed was empty and the house was already buzzing. Sandra met me in the hall and gave me a hug. "Good morning." I squeezed a bit tighter.

"Good morning. You need to talk to your daughter. She won't get dressed."

"OK, but I need to put some coffee on first."

Coffee on, I made my way to Emma's room. "Baby girl, you need to get dressed."

"I don't have any clean clothes." I could tell she had been crying.

"What? Yes, you do. You've got a closet full of clothes. Here, wear your wolf shirt."

"I can't wear that one."

"Why not? You love this shirt."

"The other kids make fun of me. And some of the boys hit me."

"They hit you? For wearing a wolf shirt? Is it because of the tail? Because I can cut that off."

"No, don't. I just don't want to wear it to school."

"I'm sorry, babe. Sometimes kids are assholes. And wearing shirts with tails gives assholes an excuse to be mean. But you can wear your wolf shirt at home. It can be your new pajama shirt. So, how about your robot shirt? Is that one OK?"

"Yeah, it's OK."

I hadn't noticed that David was listening.

"Dad, do the kids in the school hit the other kids?"

"Sometimes." I didn't want to lie to the boy.

"Do I have school next week?" There was fear in his eyes.

"No, honey, not until after the summer break."

"When I am at school, will you still pick me up?"

"Sure, at least for the first few weeks until you get used to the new place. But you're a big boy and the school is pretty close, so you can walk home by yourself like your sister does. But come on, let's have breakfast. We can talk about that stuff later."

The kids followed me to the kitchen. I grabbed a cup of coffee and joined them at the table. Emma still had red eyes. David was quiet. I took a sip and knew I would miss those naked, schoolyard children.

Lecture Notes on Fandom

The European Football Championship has started, and once again I am at a loss in my attempt to understand fandom. Now, it's not that I don't understand why people are fans of teams. That part I get. Mostly. What I don't understand is why they insist on waking up my children with their celebrations.

Somehow fandom grants the right to annoy. But how? The logic escapes me.

"I am happy that my country's team won. Therefore, I am going to drive around Rob's neighborhood and wake up his children with my honking and yelling."

The philosopher in me knows what this kind of reasoning is called. It's a *non sequitur*. But it's the citizen in me that knows what it really is. It's madness. It's tolerated madness, normalized madness, socially acceptable madness, but it's madness just the same.

And it's hard to explain this madness to my children. 'Dad, what's going on?' they will say to me, standing in the hall clutching a stuffed animal.

"I'm sorry, honey," I'll reply. "But some millionaires with nice asses and short shorts pretended to get hurt and then kicked a ball and now drunk people are happy. Go to sleep. It'll be over soon." I'll say this because I have a strict no-lying-to-children policy.

Of course, the game itself is not madness, nor is watching it and having a good time. If you want to get loud in a stadium or sports bar, be my guest. I like games. I even play games.

Well, I play video games. Lots of video games.

There's no particular genre of video game that I like more than any other, but the ones I truly love do have one thing in common: they are hard. Mastering a hard game gives me a kind of satisfaction, perhaps similar to the satisfaction sports fans feel when their team accomplishes something similarly challenging. But, imagine if I were allowed to express my satisfaction in the same way: wandering around my neighborhood with an air horn and blasting the Super Mario Bros. theme song.

"All you kids need to wake the hell up, because this guy just beat the original Super Mario Bros. on original hardware in less than 6 minutes!"

I would be arrested. Perhaps rightly so.

But, now that I think about it, my analogy isn't quite right. If I beat a hard game, or do a challenge run of a not-so-hard game, and then feel that satisfaction that comes with accomplishment, it's because of something I did. My skills. My talent. My satisfaction. But the football fans? They haven't done anything other than drink beer and watch men with nice asses play. So, really, if I follow the logic, I should be able to wake the neighborhood kids up after watching some Street Fighter gameplay videos on YouTube, provided that those Youtubers have nice asses.

"Out of bed, kids! I just watched Daigo parry a 30-hit combo in Street Fighter IV and go on to win the Ouka Ranbu Cup!"

Again, arrested. This time definitely rightly so.

Geek 5.0

I hated my seventh grade science teacher. Despite being the best student in his class, he never wasted an opportunity to humiliate me. I still don't know why he did it. I think he liked me well enough — he said as much to my mother at a parent-teacher conference. Maybe he thought his actions would motivate me. Maybe he didn't know how to express his feelings. Or, maybe, he was just an asshole.

Looking back, I favor the latter theory. Now that I am a teacher myself, I know there are times when I embarrass students, but it's always playful, never sadistic, and only when they do something wrong — come in late, don't do the homework, check their phones in class. A joke at their expense can bring them in line. Make them better students. And, most importantly, entertain me while I'm working.

The only things I did wrong in seventh grade were

being the new kid and being poor in a rich school district.

When we took tests, he would walk up and down the rows making sure we weren't cheating. On one such test day, he stopped at my table, reached down, and pinched my sweatpants. He rolled the purple material between his fingers. "Three ninety-nine," he said.

The class turned to look.

"What?" I said.

"Three ninety-nine at Big Lots. The cheapest sweatpants money can buy."

The class sniggered.

"I don't know how much they cost," I said and turned back to my test, hopping the burning feeling didn't indicate I had a red face.

He walked off with a spring in his step, and because the universe is unjust, he didn't fall and break his nose.

That was the last time I wore those sweatpants to school. Before that day they were my favorite because they reminded me of the Incredible Hulk. But, despite my fondness, they stayed at home. I didn't want to hear another comment.

And, because I lacked the Hulk's ability to turn anger into preternatural strength, I didn't want him to have an excuse to touch me again.

The science classroom was on the side of the building that ran parallel to the playground. A half-hour before classes ended, the street that ran through the playground was opened so parents could line up in their cars to pick up their kids. So, while we were still fingers deep in dissected frogs, we could watch the cars coming in. When the first started to arrive, we knew class was almost over, which was an exciting time for most.

I didn't have to look to know when my mom arrived. I could hear it. In those days, she drove a rusty 1968 Chevy Nomad, my step-father called it the 'Go-mad,' and it was loud—partly because of the big engine, but mostly because we didn't have the money to replace the muffler.

"Hey, Rob, your mom is here in her grocery-getter a bit early today," my teacher announced to the class.

"How do you know it's my mom?" I asked, trying to sound unfazed by the insinuation.

"Whose else would it be?"

The class sniggered.

Near the end of the semester, a cop car pulled into the playground. A few classmates glanced up and then returned to their work. I caught the eye of the class's only black student, himself a recent addition to the school, his family having relocate to Whitehall from Muskegon Heights. We exchanged glances. He shrugged his shoulders and grimaced before returning to his reading.

Perhaps noticing our exchange, the science teacher broke the silence. "You can tell which side of society you're on by how you feel when you see a police officer." He glanced in my direction but made no further comment.

Snippets of overheard conversations replayed in my mind.

My step-father to my mother: "You follow me in your car and keep close. My tags are expired."

My mother to my step-father: "Slow down before you hit Cherry Street. That cop likes to sit behind those bushes and we don't have insurance."

My uncle to my brother: "I was just walking home. I wasn't hurting anybody. I left my car at the bar for a reason. Now I have to pay them for sleeping in the tank when they could have just let me walk home. Fuckers."

My step-mother to my father: "Well, what are we going to do? We can't pay this ticket and get the boys a Nintendo."

My father to no one in particular: "I don't know."

But the conversation that stuck out the most in my memory was the one I was a part of. I heard our neighbor screaming at my mother through the apartment's paper-thin walls: "And don't even think about stepping outside, Martha! I don't want to see you or those kids in the yard. You know what I can do!"

I didn't know why she was mad at us, and I didn't know what she could do. I couldn't imagine my mom doing anything to inspire that kind of enmity. Mom was one of the nicest people I had ever met. "What are we going to do, Mom?" I asked.

"Just go in your room and play." She looked down at the newspaper on the table, but I could tell she wasn't reading it. Her jaw was set in the same clinched position that proceeded the fifth time she would tell my brother and I to please stop fighting.

With a clearly unhinged neighbor yelling through the walls, we could have used a cop, but the thought of calling a one didn't cross my mother's mind.

It was strange that I hadn't thought of it before, but after the question was posed by the asshole science teacher, it was obvious: Grow up poor in America, grow up fearing the police.

Twenty-five years later, and with poverty and America's cops long behind me, I still wasn't too excited when Mateo called me and asked if I could take over teaching his English class at the local police department. Their computer forensics department was looking for an English teacher who cold help them prepare for training seminars, and he didn't have time to do it again.

"You'll like them," Mateo said. "Some of them are really good and they're motivated."

"I don't want to be in a room with motivated cops," I replied.

"Don't be silly. Their office is within walking distance of your apartment. Roll out of bed and you're nearly there."

I sighed. "I do like walking to work, but still, I'm going to have to pass."

"They're more computer geeks than cops. They don't wear uniforms, they like to talk about video games and comic books. You'll like them."

"Well, I do like talking about video games, but still, no. They're cops."

"They pay very well and Sony's new VR headset looks really cool." Mateo was always good at arguing his point.

"OK, fine. If people within walking distance want to pay me to talk about video games and teach a little grammar, I guess I'm not going to say no. Even if they are cops."

Shortly after the phone call, Mateo sent me the contact email for the department and a copy of the bill he had used so I knew what they expected. For a moment I considered making a new email account to use for my police communications, but my laziness trumped whatever trepidations were lurking in my psyche.

After hitting the send button, I started to read up on the forthcoming comic books, and just as I started to see what the Hulk would be up to in the coming months, I got an email from the contact person in the police, Dieter.

I was struck and impressed by his promptness and polite yet informal tone. He told me that if it fit with my schedule, I could stop by the following day after lunch for a chat about the course. I sent him a response telling him I could be there at one o'clock.

The next day after my university classes, I headed over to the city's main police campus. Unlike the police station downtown, which served the public, the campus area was where the investigative units were located. The whole area was fenced in and, decidedly, not open to the public. The only way in was through the guard station. I approached the gate, waved at the guards in the booth, one of them buzzed me in and another, somewhat smaller one, stepped outside and turned towards me.

"Hi. I'm Rob McGee. I have an appointment with the computer forensics department," I said in German, and then we shook hands.

"Are you here for an interview?" he asked, also in German.

"No. I'm the new English teacher."

"Oh, you're the English teacher?"

"That's me." I smiled.

"So, you don't speak German then?"

My smile disappeared. Our entire conversation had taken place in German so I wasn't exactly sure how to respond. If he didn't think I spoke German, how could we have gotten this far in the conversation? Further, if he didn't think I spoke German, why did he ask me a question in German? My mind started racing for a solution. Maybe, I thought, it was a kind of logic puzzle. We were speaking German, but I couldn't speak German. Could both of those propositions be true at the same time? Maybe. But that line of reasoning would either violate the law of excluded middle, or turn me into one of Searle's Chinese Rooms. So that was a dead end. It had to be something else. Could Grice help? Was this police officer flouting the rules of logic while still wanting to communicate somehow? If yes, then there had to be some hidden conversational implicature. But what was it? What was he trying to say?

He looked up at my face, which I assume looked confused—it's easy to assume a face contorted by the weighing of communication theories expresses confusion. "Wait, no, sorry," he said. "That doesn't make any sense." And then he giggled a bit to himself.

I exhaled.

"So, who's your contact person?"

"I don't remember. Let me check my email." I reached into my pocket and pulled out my phone, and since this happened in Germany and not America, I didn't get shot five times.

I pulled up the email and showed it to the officer. "Here it is. His name is Dieter Schmitt."

He read through the email and nodded. "OK. Do you know where you need to go?"

"No, not really. First day."

He smiled. "Follow this road until you see a tunnel. Go through the tunnel and turn left. Their building is at the end of that road on the right. Or, I can call someone to come get you."

"That's nice of you, but I think I can find it. Thank you."

"Have a good day, Mr. McGee." He extended his hand.

We shook, again. "You, too." My smile returned.

Finding the building was easy enough, and after being buzzed in, I was greeted by a rather large man with Buddy Holly glasses and an unbuttoned red gingham shirt, which was presumably unbuttoned to show off the Marilyn Manson t-shirt underneath. He introduced himself as Mathias and after I explained who I was, he smiled broadly and switched to English. "Good to meet you. Dieter told me we would be having English classes again. Do we start today?"

"No, not today. I'm just here to talk to Dieter about the class."

"Oh, OK. Do you know where his office is?"

"No."

"He's up on the third floor. It's the third office on the right. I think." He looked to be imagining the hallway. "Third or fourth, but it doesn't matter. His name is on the door. Should I take you up?"

"I'm sure I can find it OK, but thank you," I said.

"No problem. See you around."

"For sure."

I walked up the stairs and started to relax a little. I didn't think I could hate an adult fan of Marilyn Manson. A teenage fan trying to shock a parent, sure, but not an adult.

Upstairs I found Dieter's office, it was the fifth door on the right so apparently Mathias was pretty bad at spacial reasoning. I knocked and heard a voice telling me to come in.

The room wasn't small by any means, but was mostly desk, one of those three-sided monstrosities, and every inch of it was covered in either neat stacks of papers or random computer parts. The man with closely shaved white hair sitting behind the desk was not wearing a rock-band t-shirt, but still looked friendly enough. I introduced myself and he smiled.

He made his way around the desk and extended his hand. "Thanks for coming in on such short notice. Please, have a seat." He motioned to a small table in the corner, the only surface in the room not covered by work. I sat down and took out a little notebook. Dieter took a seat opposite.

"Did you have any trouble getting through the guard station?" he asked.

"Nothing a little philosophical training couldn't solve," I said.

He scrunched up his face."Oh, did they give you a hard time?"

"No, it was OK. The guard was a little confused at first, but we figured it out."

"Good. I told them you would be coming, but they don't pay much attention to email. I'm sure that after a few weeks, you'll just be able to wave and they'll buzz you through."

"Cool." I nodded and opened my notebook. "So, tell me about the class. What do you need? What skill level are the participants? How often would you like to meet?"

Dieter walked me through what they were looking for. Most of it was what every client wants: more practice with conversation, a little help with grammar, vocabulary exercises. He also hopped I could help with police vocabulary as it related to investigations and computer crimes. This did sound more interesting than my normal classes, but it also sounded like I would have to do some research myself. I wasn't worried about my computer knowledge, but I knew nothing about police work — aside from what I had picked up from watching The Wire, of course. Throughout the conversation, Dieter confused me a few times and I looked up to see a sly grin. I wasn't prepared for his sarcasm. As the conversation went on, against my better judgment, I liked him.

Our conversation wound to a close and I put my notebook away. "Mateo sent me a copy of the bill he used when he worked for you. Should I bring mine with me on the first class?"

"You could. But if you've already prepared one, you could give it to me now."

"Yeah, I've got one with me." I dug through my bag until I found my business classes folder, and then handed him the bill.

"Thanks for the bill, Rob. I'll be sure to throw this in the trash when I have time." He put the bill on a stack of papers on his desk and smiled.

"Be careful, Dieter. If I don't get my money, I'll have to call the police."

He shook his head and giggled. "Come on, let me show you around." We exited his office and he gave me a brief tour, the most important bit for me was the meeting room we would use as a classroom. With a whiteboard, digital projector, and small clutch of computers in the corner, it was better equipped for teaching that my room at the university, so I couldn't complain.

When we made it back to his office, he thanked me again for coming by on such short notice and we said our goodbyes. As I made my way past the guard tower, I started to think about activities for the course. I wasn't worried about teaching grammar or basic conversation skills, of course—I could talk about verb tenses, sentence structure, and commas for hours. My problem with this course was that I didn't know anything about police work.

As I made my way home, I realized that this wasn't so different from when I started teaching at the bank. Back then I didn't know anything about banking, so I brought in articles about the financial crisis and made the bankers explain to me why some other bankers thought it was a good idea to engage in gambles that could potentially destroy the world's financial sectors. They tried to explain it, I filled in missing vocabulary, and we made a class out of it.

I considered following a similar strategy with the police, but didn't think it would be effective. My bankers read the financial press for fun, so helping them through newspaper articles they wanted to read anyway was a good way to keep them interested. I didn't imagine that police who thought Marlyn Manson t-shirts were suitable work attire would be terribly interested in newspaper articles about police investigations. Especially considering the fact that many American newspaper articles about the police were about how they killed more than one-thousand people a year and never faced any consequences.

I needed something that appealed to their police needs, their geeky side, and would allow me to figure out where the gaps were in their English. When I got home, I sat on the sofa and looked down at the pile of toys my son had left on the living room floor, and the solution became obvious. Who is the most brilliant detective ever and is well-loved by those of the geeky persuasion?

Batman was the answer.

The idea was simple: modern superhero comic books are drawn in a way such that the story is quite clear without the dialog—if you forced my hand, I'd say we have Jack Kirby to thank for this style of storytelling even though others might insist on Will Eisner, but I digress. So, my plan was to buy some

Batman comics, leave the first few pages as is to set up the story and then remove the text from the rest of the dialog bubbles. The students would then read the first few pages to get into the story and then fill in the missing dialog on their own. By picking a Batman comic, especially if I could find one that involved him investigating a crime, they'd have to use investigation vocabulary and conversational speech to finish the book. I could then walk around, ask them to describe the scenes they were working on, and help with whatever knowledge gaps they might have.

All in all, a rather brilliant idea (and if any Marvel or DC executives are reading this and thinking about producing a series of comics for language learners, I would encourage you to do so, and I would also encourage you to pay me for the idea).

For the briefest of moments, I considered using some of my books, but the thought of other people touching my comics pushed that notion out of my head. A quick glance at the clock told me I had plenty of time before the comic book shop closed and since it was a Thursday, I didn't even have to worry about picking up the kids. Thursdays were Grandma-days, which also meant that they were normally Rob-plays-videos-games-in-his-pajamas days, but I was willing to make an exception since it meant I had an excuse to hang out in a local comic book shop. I grabbed my headphones, loaded up a Marilyn Manson album, and headed downtown.

The comic book shop was relatively empty, which wasn't unexpected. There were a few girls looking at manga, an obvious parent searching for a gift, and a couple of twenty-somethings mulling about, but that wasn't enough to clog up the aisles, which was good. I nodded at one of the employees, but made no effort to engage in a stop-and-chat. The people who worked there were nice enough, I'd even invited one of them over to my place to play video games once, but I didn't feel like talking about superheroes or whatever new Star Wars movie was coming out. My geeky interests aside, I wasn't a geek. I could talk about other things and I, on occasion, put my penis inside a woman's mouth. The headphones stayed on.

Most of their comic stock was in German, which was useless to me, but they did have a decent selection of original English comics stashed away in long boxes in the back under a shelf of lewd vinyl statues of anime girls in various states of undress. For their sakes, I hopped the Toy Story universe wasn't real.

After a shudder, I started looking through the Batman boxes. The story wasn't relevant, I just need one that had pictures of Batman looking around a crime scene, maybe putting stuff into little plastic bags, or, in Batman's case, into his utility belt. I also didn't want to spend very much money, so the sought-after books were ignored in favor of throw-away stories nobody remembered. To this end, I was digging through books from the nineties. After a while, my back and knees started to protest the frog position I was in, so I pulled the long box out and sat down next to it on the floor. The floor was still a pretty uncomfortable place to be with legs as long as mine, but it was better than bending over. Once I started to make a mess, an employee to come back and see what I was doing with their stock.

"Can I help you find something?" I barely heard over Marilyn screaming.

I took off my headphones and looked back over my shoulder. "Sure, have a seat. I'm looking for a few books that show Batman walking around a crime scene — taking pictures, collecting samples, stuff like that."

"Oh, hey, Rob. I didn't recognize you down there. I don't think I've seen the top of your head before."

"No, I suppose you haven't. You don't climb up on chairs often enough for that."

He chuckled and sat down. "So, any particular issue?"

"No, I just need some artwork of a crime scene for a project—bonus points if he's talking to someone at the same time, so maybe something with Robin." I paused my music and pulled out a few promising issues. We chatted about Batman and the new Star Wars movie, and I found myself wishing I was better at remembering names. You can only say 'Hey, man' so many times before they realize you don't know.

Together we found a number decent options. I pulled out a few from the shortlist with admirable artwork by Tim Sale and we cleaned up my mess. Five comics richer and six euros poorer, I stepped outside and unlocked my bike. Even though it was only five o'clock, it was already getting dark. Winter in Southern Germany. What they make up for with a lack of snow is a lack of sun. I wasn't sure if it was a good deal, but at least I could use my bike nearly year-round.

On my way home, I stopped by the grocery store to pick up some dinner for me the kids and a few essentials for myself, a six-pack of beer and a bottle of bourbon. By the time I got out of the store, the sun had given up any pretense of sticking around. Like the office workers, the winter sun in Germany was a nine-to-fiver and wasn't terribly interested in overtime.

Since I lived more-or-less downtown, I didn't have to worry about not being able to see the sidewalk, plenty of streetlights along Mainzer street, but when I turned down the alley that connected to my apartment, things weren't so bright. I could hear some glass crunching under my tires but didn't worry about it too much—Sandra had paid a bit extra for puncture-proof tires, which was a good investment since we lived near an abandoned parking structure next to a seldom-visited strip club, the kind of area that attracted people who didn't care as much for the bottle deposit as they did for the sound of glass breaking.

Just on the other side of the alley, I zipped across the street and into the little driveway that connected the private park behind our apartment to the street. Just as I made the corner, I hit the brakes. Hard. My neighbor started screaming at me. "Watch out! What do you think you are doing? Why don't you have lights on your bike?"

"Sorry, Mr. Klein. I didn't see you there," I said.

"It's illegal to ride at night without lights."

"Sorry," I said again. Mr. Klein and I had an uncomfortable history and I didn't want to instigate anything. He had once knocked on my door and asked if I could control my cat better, and I said, 'No, he's a cat.' Well, Mr. Klein didn't like that answer very much so I asked him what he would like me to do. He went on to complain that Ziggy had gotten locked in his cellar and had once darted into his apartment. He further explained that his son had a rather extreme cat allergy, so having a cat rubbing himself on their stuff was undesirable. 'OK,' I had replied, 'but what should I do about it?' Again, Mr. Klein repeated the allergy concerns which didn't answer my question and suggested to me that he wasn't capable of having reasonable conversations at all, so I said, 'Well, if my cat rubbing on your stuff is a problem, then maybe you shouldn't lock him in your cellar or let him into your apartment,' and Mr. Klein really didn't like that response so he huffed off. A few days later we got a letter from the owners of the apartment building telling us that if we didn't control our cat, we'd have to get rid if him. And then it was Sandra's turn to be mad at me.

I made a motion to go around Mr. Klein and he stepped in front of me. "Something else bothering you, Mr. Klein?"

"No." He made no attempt to get out of my way.

In my mind, I stepped off my bike and showed Mr. Klein why it was a bad idea to annoy guys twice his size, but then my mind informed me that he was the kind of man to hide behind relevant authorities: a neighbor breaks the house rules, the landlord gets a letter; a neighbor breaks the law, the police get called. I certainly didn't want to deal with the cops, so I backed up a bit and the made a wide pass of Mr. Klein.

A few days later, it was time to teach the police again, and so, with Batman comics in my messenger bag, I walked over to the guard station. As I got closer, it was clear that I would have to talk to new guards. Apparently, the exciting job of protecting a parking lot and buildings full of people with guns was rotated with some regularity.

And so, again, I had to explain who I was and what I was doing there. Fortunately, the guard of the day didn't seem to think I was much of a threat, probably because he recognized I wouldn't be able to run very fast in leather-soled brogues. So, after asking if I knew where I was supposed to go, he waved me through and returned to his chair.

After getting buzzed into the computer forensics lab, I made my way to the meeting room on the third floor, saying hi to a few of the officers in the break room on my way. The projector was still on in the meeting room and the screensaver had kicked in. A 3D sentence bounced around the screen: 'Gotta catch 'em all!'

Given where I was, I wasn't sure if it was a reference to Pokémon or police work. Probably both. With a nod to the clever slogan, I hit the power button and wrote the day's lesson on the board.

The students filed in and took their seats. Being the first day, I had them introduce themselves and tell me about their hobbies and interests. I made mental notes of pronunciation issues, grammar problems, and the unforgivable aesthetic opinion of thinking Tolkien was a great writer.

After the warm-up, I steered the class into a short conversation about police work. I played the role of being completely ignorant about German law, which didn't require much acting skill, and asked them about various crimes I had heard of which were new to me. For example, I had heard that it was illegal in Germany to flip people off (the Germans have a wonderful word for this by the way. *Stinkefinger ziegen*, to show someone the stink-finger), and since I had wanted to do this on a number of occasions, I was curious to know if it was true.

Unfortunately it was true, at least in certain circumstances. Drivers were not permitted to show other drivers the stink-finger, the idea being that cars are dangerous and it's not a good idea to make people in dangerous objects angry. I had to admit it made some sense. But still, some drivers need to be reminded that they are assholes, so I couldn't agree with the law whole-heartedly. Maybe if bad drivers saw enough stink-fingers, they would recognize the obvious truth: they were assholes who would do well to adjust their behavior for polite driving society. But maybe I was just a middle-finger optimist. Or maybe I was such a dedicated teacher that I recognized even a carefully chosen finger could be a teaching tool.

Showing police and other state officials the stink-finger, I learned, was the other disallowed circumstance. I didn't ask, but assumed the reasoning was similar: police and bureaucrats with official stamps are dangerous, so it's not a good idea to make them angry.

But, the upshot was, as far as I could tell, I didn't have to give up all hope of using my middle finger in Germany. I just needed a teachable moment, something outside of a car and not in front of a state employee.

I went to the whiteboard and wrote 'Crime Scene' in the middle and circled it. "OK, let's think about things we see or do at a crime scene."

The class offered various ideas: victim, blood, computers, evidence bags, cameras, poor people, et cetera. I circled those words and asked further questions about them. "What is important on the computer?", "What does blood smell like?", "Why are poor people worse at crime than politicians?" and so on. After the board was more-or-less full, I opened my bag and pulled out the Batman comics. A few of the students shifted in their seats to get a better view. I had seen those expressions before. My kids made the same faces when I came home with a bag from the comic book shop.

I explained what we were going to do with the comics as I passed them around the room. "Read the beginning to get an idea of the story, and then work together with a partner to fill in as much of the missing text as you can. Don't write in the books. The missing sections are numbered. You can use those numbers on your own piece of paper to stay organized."

Once they started, I walked around the room to help.

"Hey, Rob," Mathias the Marilyn Manson fan said, "I know it doesn't have anything to do with what we're doing, but why don't the bad guys in Gotham just light the bat-signal and wait for Batman to show up? Seems like a good way to ambush him."

It was a good question, but one that every Batman fan knew the answer to. "Because they are afraid of him," I said. "Batman capitalizes on their fears. He's a big guy in a bat costume who has a tool and a plan for every situation—he's even bested Superman on a number of occasions. The last place a criminal wants to be when the bat-signal gets turned on is on that rooftop."

He nodded, satisfied with my answer. "I wish we had a bat-signal."

"It wouldn't work without a Batman," I said. "If you want to scare Germans, you should make a light to call the tax office."

He giggled and turned back to the comic.

Before long, I instructed the class to stop writing and asked for a few volunteers to read what they had written. Their creativity was impressive, especially Mathias's pun-filled offering. After offering a few corrections, we moved on to a discussion about crime scenes they had been involved with, and then class was over.

The next morning, Sandra woke me up with a concerned voice. "Rob, you need to look outside. I think somebody stole your bike tire."

"Are you serious?" I threw my legs over the bed and grabbed my robe from the bench that held my not-quite-clean, but not-quite-dirty, clothes pile.

"I think it's your bike. I thought you might need more time to get to work if it is."

"I don't work today. The bankers canceled."

"Oh, sorry. I didn't know."

I nodded at her explanation for interrupting my hangover sleep and gave her a hug. "Good thinking. And good morning."

She squeezed. "Good morning."

I went to the kitchen and turned on my coffee maker, and then walked out onto the balcony. My bike was chained up under it and when I leaned out over the edge, I saw the back forks resting metallically on the concrete. I gripped the railing a bit tighter and grimaced. "Fuckers."

"So, is it yours?" Sandra asked when I came back in.

"Yep."

"Assholes."

"Yeah, I was thinking something along those lines as well." I grabbed a cup from the cabinet stood in front of my coffee machine waiting until enough had dripped out to fill the cup.

"Our insurance should pay for a new one," Sandra said after I had taken a few sips. "I'm sure we'll need a police report for that to work though."

"I don't know how to do that, and I don't really want to call the police."

"Call your students. Maybe they can do it for you."

"Worth a shot."

I finished my cup of coffee and called Dieter. After explaining the situation, he told me I'd have to go to the downtown police station to file the report. I thanked him and hung up.

Sandra came in with one of her folders and flipped through until she found what she wanted. I recognized the letterhead as our insurance company's. She called the hotline and, after waiting on hold for a few minutes, asked what we would need to file the claim. As expected, we needed a police report, we also needed pictures and a receipt from the repair.

"OK," I said. "I'll throw on some clothes and take some pictures. The police might want those, too."

Outside, I snapped a few pictures and was about to unlock my bike and carry it to the bike shop when I heard someone approach. I stood up and turned. Mr. Klein. "Problems with your bike?" This was a typical way for Saarlanders to initiate a conversation: ask a question about something completely obvious. In the grocery store, they might ask if you are shopping; in the park, they might ask if you are enjoying the sun; or at the doctor's they might ask if you are finally going to have that lump looked at.

"No. Everything is fine," I said flatly.

He smiled without kindness and I thought there was a decent possibility he had stolen my tire. But since I didn't have any evidence and suspected that cops wouldn't be interested in dusting for fingerprints for something as minor as a bike tire, I didn't dwell on that possibility for long. Mr. Klein walked over to the dumpsters and threw away the bag he was carrying. I unlocked my bike, strained a bit under its weight, wished for a moment that I had gone with a normal bike instead of the much heavier e-bike, and walked out of the courtyard.

At the bike shop, I put the bike down and waited for employee to finish with a customer. I recognized the worker as the one who had sold me the bike. He was quite tall for a German, so it was nice talking to him; I didn't have to look down. After the customer left, he walked around the counter. "You're missing something," he said with a sympathetic grin.

"Yeah, I think the thieves needed some parts to build a unicycle."

He laughed and shook his head.

"So if you see some shady clowns around town, let me know."

"I can do that." He bent down to take a closer look. "I think I've got a tire for this in the back."

"That's good news. How long do you think it'll take?"

"I can get to it today. You can pick it up this afternoon."

I nodded and looked around the shop. Boxes of various bike lights hung on the opposite wall. "Hey, since I'm here, can you put some lights on for me?"

"Sure. Which ones do you want?" He motioned and walked over to their selection.

"I want the brightest front light I'm allowed to have."

"That would be this set." He handed me a box. The lights were on the expensive side, but I wasn't a poor kid in Michigan anymore, and besides, buying electronics always made me feel better. I nodded. "OK. I might need a bit more time to do the lights as well, so how about you stop by just before we close."

"Sounds good." I handed the box back to him.

He took the box back to the counter and jotted down some notes on a slip of paper, a work-order, I guessed. We shook hands and said our goodbyes. Now, I just had the police to deal with.

The police station was in the same neighborhood as the bank I taught at, so there was no need to look up the address; I had walked past it many times. When I got to the corner opposite the station, a few police officers came out and lit up cigarettes. I turned left and walked around the block. By the time I had circled back, the entrance was free, so I went in.

It was the first time I had been in a police station voluntarily, but despite the fact I wasn't being forced to be there, I tensed up. My eyes darted around the room. The inside was the same lifeless brown that I had come to expect from German offices. At the far end of the room, a tan padded bench wrapped around the inside corner. A few magazines were strewn across a little table in front of the bench. It almost looked like something from a dentist's office. To the right of the door a bored looking cop sat behind a desk. He looked up over his moustache. "Can I help you?"

I swallowed. "Yes, my bike tire was stolen, and I would like to file a report."

"Where's the bike now?"

"At the bike shop."

He frowned and shook his head.

"Is that a problem?"

"You are supposed to leave it where the crime occurred until we take pictures."

"Oh, I didn't know that. I talked to a police officer and he told me to come here. He didn't say anything about leaving my bike at home. But, I did take some pictures."

He puffed out his cheeks with an exhaled breath while rocking his head from side to side. "OK. Have a seat." He nodded towards the bench.

A short while later a female officer came out from one of the side doors and helped me fill out the report. She explained with an understanding smile that there wasn't much hope of recovering the tire and I told her I didn't care about the tire and certainly didn't expect the police to look for it, but, all the same, I needed a report for my insurance. "Oh," she said, "well, then I'll type this up and send it out to you today."

"That would be great. Do you need the pictures?"

"Yes. You can email them to me at this address." She handed me a card.

"Thanks. I'll send them right away."

"OK. Anything else we can do for you, Mr. McGee?"

"No, I don't think so. Thank you."

"Have a good day."

As soon as I got outside, I emailed the pictures. I

looked back at the police station wondering why I had found the place so intimidating before, and then walked down the street to grab a sandwich and a beer.

After going grocery shopping that evening, I stopped by the bike shop. They had managed to finish everything, so I didn't have to walk the rest of the way home. When I got to the alley, I hit the button for the lights and the whole street was lit up. A smile was plastered on my face as I slalomed around the glittering piles of broken beer bottles.

I darted across the street and into the courtyard behind my apartment. As I made the corner, Mr. Klein raised his hands in front of his face, and I hit the brakes. "Get that light out of my face!" he wailed.

I extended my middle finger and put my hand into the beam of my headlight. An impressive shadow was thrown across Mr. Klein and onto the wall behind him.

A bat-signal for assholes.

Celebrate Christmas the German Way, with a Belly Full of Chestnuts and a Heart Full of Fear

Dear Friends,

My wife Sandra and I were wandering the forests on the hunt for chestnuts a few weeks back when she noticed there were no chestnut trees to be found. A quick Internet search told us that the American chestnut trees were wiped out by a blight some 70 years ago. "Well," she said, "'blight' is a pretty cool word, but we can't have Christmas dinner without chestnuts." It was then that the idea hit us: if our American friends have been missing out on chestnuts, maybe they have been missing out on other European traditions as well, maybe we should invite them over for some Old World Christmas charm.

So, that's what we are doing. On Friday, December 21st, we hope you are yours will join us and ours for coffee, cake, and a few very special Christmas visitors from the old country.

We'll start promptly at 4:00 with *Stollen*, which is Germany's version of fruitcake. We've had American fruitcake and invite you to set your prejudices aside and give the *Stollen* a try; it really is something special. It looks like a loaf of bread with a fat center and tapered edges, and this shape is no baking accident. It is intended to represent the shape of baby Jesus, wrapped in swaddling clothes, about to be baked at 300 degrees for 15 to 20 minutes. Just one heavenly bite and you'll feel the hand of God gently caressing your stomach. Almost literally.

After coffee and cake, we will be visited by none other than Saint Nicolas himself. One thing you are sure to notice is that the German Santa has a few helpers—and I'm not talking about elves. No, in Germany, Santa is accompanied by altogether different sorts of characters, one of whom is Knecht Ruprecht. He will be easily recognizable by his brown robe, black beard, and that magical twinkle he gets in his eyes when Santa instructs him to beat a naughty child with a cane.

We know, of course, that the American Santa leaves

naughty children a lump of coal instead of toys as punishment, and we admire the fact that the American Santa doles out punishment himself. He's a go-getter, that American Santa. In Europe, St. Nicolas has outsourced the punishment job. I suppose it's not unlike how the American Santa has outsourced the toy building to the elves. And, just as Santa's elves are happy to build toys for the deserving American child, Santa's Knecht Ruprecht is happy to beat the undeserving child to within an inch of his life, stuff him into a burlap bag, and throw him into an icy river, where he will, presumably, drown. So, the traditions are quite similar when you think about it.

But don't worry too much about Knecht Ruprecht. He really is a kind soul who has your children's best interests at heart. If they survive the icy water, they will wander back to the party flecked with bruises but full of remorse and holiday cheer.

That being said, you should worry about the Krampus.

In the Alpine regions Germany, Santa's entourage includes not only the cane-happy, child-beating Knecht Ruprecht, but also something sinister—a half-goat, half-demon monster called the Krampus. Like Knecht, the Krampus has a taste for torturing children, but unlike Knecht, when the Krampus carts the children away, they don't normally come back. We've heard rumors that they are eaten, and we've heard other rumors that they are dragged straight to Hell itself, but the truth is we don't know what happens. All that we do know is that those children who *do* come back are changed into the perfect Christmas party guests. Sure, they return with dull and lifeless eyes, but that lost twinkle returns as soon as the Christmas tree is set ablaze with the fire of celebration. Christmas is a magical time in Germany.

We would love to share this magical holiday with you, our American friends. There's no need to bring anything, but the children should wear comfortable, warm clothes and shoes suitable for running through the snow for their very lives.

Merry Christmas and Frohe Weihnachten!
Rob and Sandra

Talking to a Wall

When Emma didn't listen, we blamed it on the fact that she was becoming a teenager. When David didn't listen, we blamed it on the fact that he was a five-year-old boy. But when he nearly ripped the skin off of his penis, Sandra and I figured it was time we stop denying the problem and take a more pro-active approach to parenting. Up until that point, the kids not listening had caused a certain amount of grief, but a bloody penis does wonders to motivate parents out of the denial stage.

Of course, we had told him many times before that he shouldn't do gymnastics or stretching exercises when he sat on the toilet, but should just sit there without twitching, do his business, and go about his day after washing his hands, of course. Unfortunately, talking to the kids like they were humans with the capacity to understand speech was a bad strategy.

I was eating a frozen pizza when it happened. I heard some commotion in the bathroom, ignored it, and continued to enjoy how the new aioli sauce I had discovered improved Germany's already decent frozen pizzas.

And then David came in, tears in his eyes and hands crossed over his boyhood. "Daddy, I need a band-aid," he said.

I put my fork down and eyed him skeptically. "What did you do? Let me see."

"I just need a band-aid."

"You need to let me see first."

He pulled down his pants, and I didn't feel like eating pizza anymore.

Even though it wasn't bleeding too badly, it was obvious that I would have to take a closer look to investigate the damage. I told him to lie down on the sofa while I washed my hands. Despite it's salve-like texture, I was sure aioli had no business near an open wound.

When I came back in the living room, he was whimpering.

"OK, baby boy," I said. "I'm going to take a look and then get you a band-aid. OK?"

"OK."

I put one hand on his belly and pushed his penis down so I could see how extensive the injury was.

It was pretty bad.

It didn't look like the wound was very deep, but the entire top half of the penis's skin was detached from the base. A jagged half-moon rip.

"How did you do this?" I asked, trying to keep concern out of my voice.

"I fell."

I raised an eyebrow. "How did you do this by falling?"

"I just fell." He was obviously lying, but it was also obvious that he wasn't going to tell me the truth. The boy could commit to his lies, and his memory was good enough to keep his lies straight, which was an annoying combination in a child. But I consoled myself with the knowledge that if he survived childhood, he would make a decent lawyer.

"You might have to go to the doctor for this one, kiddo. Let me call your mom to get a second opinion."

A better parent would have immediately gone to a hospital, but I had grown up in the States, where hospitals were prohibitively expensive for poor families. And my family had been desperately poor. For my parents, an injury involved a calculation: How bad was it? Did it really need a doctor? Would it get better on its own? What would happen if the bill couldn't be paid? Would we lose the car? House? Food? I had heard my parents go through these calculations while I lay on the sofa bleeding or feverish.

Even though I now lived in a civilized country where a trip to the hospital cost nothing out of pocket,

I still processed injuries the way my parents had taught me to process injuries. Did it really need a doctor? Was it something we could take care of at home? Poverty had damaged my ability to assess sickness and injuries. But, I knew that it had, so I relied on Sandra's judgments.

David whimpered again. "Can I go to the doctor now? It hurts."

"I believe that. But let's wait for your mom to have a look first. She's shopping downtown with Emma and can be here soon."

"Can I have a band-aid?"

"Sure. Just give me a minute. You wanna watch TV while we wait for mom?"

He nodded weakly.

"OK, but don't move, and keep your hands out of your pants."

I sent Sandra a text telling her that she needed to come home right away and then dug through our first aid kit until I found gauze and medical tape. After taping up the wound, I admired my field dressing, and pulled his pants back up. We watched cartoons and waited for the side of the family that didn't have to worry about penile injuries to return home.

It didn't take long. And it didn't take Sandra more than a glance to decide that David needed a doctor. "That's not something we should take a chance on," she said.

"OK," I said, trusting her better judgment.

While she checked on bus times to the hospital, I sat back down with David and turned the TV off. "OK, kiddo, we're going to take you to the doctor. And when you talk to the doctor, it's important to tell him or her exactly what happened. Can you do that?"

"Yes, I can do that." He sat up. "It's not a long story. I fell."

I lowered my eyes and shook my head. The boy could commit.

Sandra came in. "So, am I taking him?"

"Oh, I thought we could all go," I said.

"We don't *all* need to go. I can do it. You can stay here and make sure Emma does her homework. Or did you *want* to go?"

"Well, no, not really. I'm just not sure which is preferable: getting Emma to do homework or explaining my son's bloody penis to strangers." I tiled my head. "Who went last time?"

"Me."

I exhaled. "Let me find some pants."

A bus ride later, David and I were in the hospital's waiting room. Like most hospitals, it smelled like disinfectant, but since we were in the children's wing, a layer of diaper sat on top of the sterile smell, and this was not an improvement. Briefly, I wondered if the geriatric ward smelled the same way.

After looking at the two magazines they had on offer, the nurse called us into an examination room. I put David on the table and opened my phone to check on a few translations. My German was pretty good, but I had never had to explain that kind of injury before.

The doctor came in. Based on how he was dressed, my first instinct was to tell him that the janitor's closet was down the hall, but then I saw the stethoscope, and closed my mouth. Until I had to explain why we were there, of course.

He instructed David to get undressed, took a quick look, and then turned back to me. "You need to go to surgery for this. It needs stitches."

I wanted to ask why he, an emergency room doctor, couldn't put in stitches, but knew it was pointless to press Germans on divisions-of-labor issues. "OK. Just point us in the right direction," I said.

He explained that we needed to go to the main entrance and sign in with the receptionist, who would be expecting us. We made our way over and signed in. The receptionist, a round woman in cat-eye glasses, gave us a room number and pointed us in the right direction with a finger that had cleavage where I expected knuckles.

Once in the room, David started to pull his pants down. "Just wait for the doctor, kiddo. It might be a bit and it's cold in here."

As soon as I finished my sentence, the door opened and a rather smiley young doctor entered. "So, who needs some stitches?" he said.

I smiled and nodded towards David, who then pulled his pants down and indicated the problem, which wasn't necessary; it was obvious enough.

The doctor stopped smiling. "OK. Well, let's have a look. Can you lay down for me?" After a prodding glance, the doctor said, "I could stitch this up, but I think glue would work better."

I wasn't sure if he was talking to himself or asking me for my opinion. "Whatever you think is best," I said.

He went with the glue.

"OK. So the glue should hold until it heals up, but keep an eye on it. You should go to your family doctor in three days to make sure everything is normal."

I nodded and thanked him.

"How did he do that by the way?" he added while David was getting dressed.

"I have no idea."

"I fell!" David butted in committedly.

***

"So, how was the doctor?" Sandra asked when we came in.

"Mommy, look. I have glue." David pulled down his pants and showed his glue.

"Does it feel better?" she asked.

"Yes. Can I watch TV?"

"No. You already watched TV today."

Sandra turned to me. "So, it went OK then?"

"Yeah, but it was a bit annoying. The emergency room doctor thought it needed stitches, but wouldn't do it. I'm not sure how you get to be an emergency room doctor without knowing how to do stitches, but what do I know? Anyway, he sent us to surgery for those, but the doctor their said glue would work if I prefered that. I also wasn't sure why a doctor would ask my opinion about something like that, but you've see which one I picked."

"Do we have to do anything?"

"No, not really. In three days we should take him to the pediatrician to check on it, but that's it."

She nodded.

"Did you get Emma to do some homework?" I asked.

"No, not really," she said, repeating my phrase. "Shortly after you guys left, my mom came over and I didn't want to deny her time with her granddaughter. So —"

"So where is Emma now?"

"She should be working in her room. Can you check on her? I have to go out. Eva and I need to finalize the schedule for the conference."

After she left, I got David situated with a TV program. Unlike Sandra, I thought a trip to the hospital warranted at least one extra episode of Pee-Wee's Playhouse. I then went to Emma's room to make sure she working.

She told me that she had finished her math and

was about to start on her reading assignment. Assuming she was telling me the truth, I went out to get a book of my own, and then joined her on her sofa.

Emma broke the silence. "Dad, what're flip-flops in English?"

"Flip-flops."

"Really?"

"Yep, it's an English word. Actually, it's an onomatopoeia, so it might have shown up in German independently, but that's pretty unlikely."

"What's an on-tomato-peea?"

"Onomatopoeia. That's a word that sounds like what it is. 'Flip-flop' is the sound your feet make when you walk in flip-flops. Flip flop, flip flop."

"My feet make the same sound. They should be called flip-flips."

I giggled. "That would work, too — putt-putt golf has a name like that. But it often flows better when the vowel sounds get a bit deeper — like tic-tac-toe. I can't even say toe-tac-tic without concentrating. 'Flip-flops' sounds good, and 'flop-flips' sounds kind of weird. If we had three feet, we'd call them flip-flap-flops."

"Nobody has three feet."

"True, but if we made flip-flops for your cat, we could call them, flip-flap-flop-flups."

She giggled. "Oh, can we do that?"

"Do what?"

"Make flip-flops for Ziggy?"

"What? No. Do your homework. Stop distracting me." Emma, like my students, had figured out it was easy to delay work by getting me to talk about language. When I noticed I had been lead astray at the university, however, I jotted down a note to remind myself to add a question about the tangent to the test. Unfortunately, I hadn't figured out a good way to apply this approach to Emma.

The book was a bit boring and I nodded off but was almost immediately woken up by the sound of Emma yelling at David. "You've watched enough for today. Turn it off."

"Dad said I could." He started to cry.

I made my way into the living room. "You are not his mother, Emma. Leave him alone."

"It's been more than an hour."

"How many times do we have to have this conversation? When will you learn that you are not his mother?"

She started to say something, but I cut her off.

"That question was rhetorical. Go to your room."

Later in the evening, after the kids were in bed, Sandra and I talked about the kids' inability to follow instructions. We didn't know what the best course of action was, so we did what we always did when we didn't know what to do: complied research. I concentrated on articles from the Anglican sphere, and Sandra the German.

The first piece of advice we decided to follow was

to give the kids simple instructions. Instead of saying things in the normal way, "David, honey, would you please put your shoes on? We're about ready to go out," we would say, "David. Shoes." It seemed a bit curt to me, but I wasn't a child psychologist so what did I know?

This technique actually worked pretty well for simple tasks — putting on shoes, brushing teeth, and so on, but was totally useless when it came to more complicated tasks like cleaning rooms, or not bossing around little brothers.

And the problem from my side with the curt approach was that it shortened my temper. Not following a polite request was one thing, but ignoring a Wittgensteinianesque language-game command indicated some sort of mental deficiency or, more probably, a desire to ignore. Since I normally doubted the former, I was forced to conclude the latter. And that was an enraging conclusion.

And thus, I entered the anger stage of parenting grief.

***

A few day ater, after a failed attempt to get David to clean his room, I stormed out. Sandra was in the hall.

She had a less-than-friendly look in her eye. "Don't just yell at him. You can't just yell at him and expect him to do it. He's five. The mess is too overwhelming."

"Yeah, exactly, he's five. If he can't put superheroes into the super-hero box and blocks into the blocks box, then I think he might be retarded and we should have him tested." I paused, looked up, and raised a finger. "And, I think I like saying 'blocks box.'"

"He's not retarded. And stop saying 'retarded'. You say it, then I think it's a normal thing for English speakers to say, so I say it, and people get mad at me. It's embarrassing." She shook her head in anger. "He just has a hard time with big projects. He's a five-year-old boy."

"I was a five-year-old boy once and I knew how to put Spider-Man in a box."

"I know your family. I'm sure you didn't have as many toys. You have to give him more specific directions."

"I don't know if I can be more specific. I've already been reduced to tautologies. Laundry goes in the laundry basket." I gestured to the left. "Books go on the bookshelf." I gestured to the right. "And finger-paintings go in the trash."

"Fine. I'll sit in there and give him directions. You help Emma practice fractions."

"Fractions?" I rubbed my head. "Do you know where I put that fifth of whisky?"

She gave me one of her looks, but, unfortunately it wasn't the look that told me where my whisky was.

Emma and I worked on fractions for a while, but when she got tired, it became impossible to get anything done. At one point she yelled at me and told me that her teacher had insisted on a different way to do a problem and refused to follow my more elegant approach.

"That's not how you do it! Mrs. Becker says it should go like this!"

"Your teacher teaches children at an elementary school. I used to teach mathematical logic at a university. You really think I don't know how to do this?"

"That's not how you do it!" She cried.

I left the room.

Sandra and I continued to read our books and parenting websites, but didn't run across any obvious solutions—in fact many of the proposed solutions were ones we'd already tried or did consistently anyway—like not backing down when faced with obstinate, disobedient children. I'd seen way too many parents fall into that trap and found them to be just as deplorable as their bratty children. What kind of person could look at themselves without shame after losing a test of wills with a five-year-old?

"So, have you run across anything interesting?" Sandra asked me one evening.

"No, not really. This book is more about why boys are falling behind in school."

"Why are you reading that?"

"I thought it might have some tips in it on how to motivate boys."

"I guess that makes sense. So, does it?"

"Yeah, but I don't see how the tips will help us with David. It talks a lot about how boys respond well to competition, but room-cleaning isn't really a competitive activity."

"Maybe it could be? We could have the kids compete to see who can clean the fastest or something."

"That might be demotivating. Emma doesn't make such extreme messes and she's a much faster cleaner, so she'd win every time."

"You're probably right." She glanced back down. "My book talks about negotiating with the children. We could try that."

"I'm not going to negotiate with children. Negotiating requires rationality and intelligence and children are irrational idiots. And plus, why would I negotiate a point I know I'm right about?"

"No, not like that." She closed her book. "More like, negotiating with perks and punishments. If they do a good job cleaning, they can negotiate a reward — a toy or a book or whatever. Or, if they don't do a good job, they can negotiate a punishment — lose an hour of TV time, no sleepover on the weekend, stuff like that. When the kids are involved in the rewards and punishments, they respond better. Apparently. They can't negotiate *out* of cleaning, but they can bargain with the consequences of doing well or poorly."

"Worth a try."

And so the bargaining stage began.

It was a colossal failure.

David said he didn't want any more toys because it would make cleaning harder if there were more things to pick up, and I was forced to reconsider my position that kids were irrational. And Emma pointed out that, under the plan, she could get stuff for not bossing her brother around by simply refusing to speak to him ever again, and that would be worse for the family than the occasional sibling fight. And so, I was forced to reconsider my position that kids were idiots.

Sandra and I both found the situation a bit depressing. She decided to do some more reading, and I decided to drink and listen to more poetry; I had recently rediscovered a CD by Steven Jesse Bernstein, an underground poet who was around during Seattle's grunge days, and I couldn't believe I kept it out of my rotation for so long.

David wandered into the living room one afternoon while I was laying on the sofa listening to a Bernstein poem about noise. "Dad, is this a song."

"No, not really." I put my drink down.

He sat next to me and listened a bit more. "Is it a story?"

"Yeah, kinda. I guess."

"So, it's a story that sounds like a song?"

"Pretty much," I said. He shuffled his feet. "Watch out, honey. I've got a drink down there."

He tilted his head and listened. "This is a story-song."

"It's called a poem, but I think Steven would have agreed with you, baby doll." David always impressed me with his creativity. When Emma didn't know a word, she'd freeze up and get frustrated, but David was always willing to coin words he thought fit the situation so he could continue the conversation. *Come on, Dad, you don't know what a flobox is? It's a robot with a dinosaur face.*

"Did you clean your room?" I asked.

"No."

"OK." I closed my eyes. David curled up with me and listened to Steven.

I woke up when Sandra came in to make David go back into his room to pick up his laundry.

"That boy," she muttered, "never fails to find a distraction."

"Just give up. It's pointless, " I said. "Like talking to a wall."

"I think a wall might listen better." She smirked. "Hmm."

"What are you hmm-ing?"

"I just had an idea."

"Let me know how that works out for you." I emptied my glass, rolled over, and drifted off.

The CD was still playing when I woke up, so I hadn't napped for long. I got up and headed towards the kitchen. I thought a few gummy bears would knock the whisky-sleep taste out of my mouth. As I passed David's room, I noticed that he had made steady progress. Sandra was in there with him, talking to a wall.

"OK, wall, now stand there and be quite. Very good wall, one point for you. OK, David, the wall has three points, and you have two. You can tie the game if you pick up your superheroes." And he did. I wasn't exactly sure what was going on.

"What are you you guys doing?" I asked.

"We're playing a game," David said.

"I see that." I turned to Sandra. "Sandra?"

"If David can follow instructions better than a wall, he can invite a friend to sleep over on the weekend."

"And this is working?"

"So far. It's like you said: competition is a good motivator. And it would be pretty embarrassing to lose a competition to a wall."

David picked up the superhero box and put it on the shelf.

"OK, wall," Sandra said, "it's a tie game. For one point, you have to make David's bed." She paused. "What? That's not how you do that. No point for you." She turned to David. "OK, David, last point. If you get it, you win. All you have to do is pick up your dirty clothes and put them in the basket."

He started to thrown his clothes in the basket. It was about the stupidest thing I had ever seen, but I couldn't argue with the results.

Later that evening, we talked about the wall technique and both agreed that there was no way Emma would fall for something so asinine, but Sandra had a different idea for her that she had read about. The plan was to all sit down together and come up with a list of house rules that we all agreed to. Having the rules written down and posted was supposed to give them weight.

"Oh, really, Frau Luther?" I said. "How many do we need? Ninety-five?"

"I think ten will be sufficient."

"I actually tried something like that when I was a kid. I was really mad at my mom about something and wrote a family constitution. I got my brother to sign it and we presented it to mom."

"How did that work out?"

"She threw it in the trash."

"That doesn't sound like your mom."

"I know. It's hard to imagine her doing that now, but we went through some stressful patches back in the day."

And so, after dinner the following evening we sat the kids down and told them the plan. We could all suggest rules and if we all agreed, we would write the rules down. The kids thought it was pretty cool to have some say in the family's management.

The first few rules were easy enough to agree to. We share, we don't hurt each other, we don't nag, everyone has to help with the housework, we don't interrupt, and so on.

"The kids should be treated the same," Emma suggested.

"No," I said, "Not the same. You're older and we can expect more from you. And you get to do more."

"That's true," Sandra added. "How about, 'The kids will be treated fairly'?"

Emma didn't seem super-happy with compromise, but she accepted and wrote it down.

We finished the list and taped it to the door in the hallway. As the weeks stretched on, Sandra and I were surprised to see that having the rules posted actually helped more than we had expected. Sure, the kids still weren't perfect angels, but referencing the rules was a faster way to diffuse situations. The rules were there. And like a man coming to terms with a terminal illness, the situation had been accepted.

Compromising Phone Calls

I try hard not to be too much of a cultural chauvinist, but some of the things Germans do are just wrong. Over the years, I've learned to tolerate all manner of behaviors that made my younger self uncomfortable: people shaking hands in non-professional contexts, people not smiling when they say hello, people not knowing how to wait in lines, et cetera. I've even adopted a few behaviors that would strike many Americans as odd: I bag my own groceries, I don't tip unless the person actually deserves it, and I can listen to political opponents without wanting them dead.

But I refuse to answer the phone by telling the caller my name.

What the Germans fail to understand is that answering the phone at home is not so different from answering the door. When I am in my pajamas, under a blanket, with a bottle of bourbon close at hand, and hear a knock at the door, I don't answer it and say, "Here is Rob." And I shouldn't be expected to answer the phone that way either.

A short 'Hello' is more than sufficient. A terse 'Who's calling?' is forgivable, and a curt 'What do you want?' is, honestly, forgivable.

Those who disturb the peace of a man in flannel pajamas should tread carefully: say hi to be nice, state a name and business, and then let him decide if the conversation is worth having.

Don't be surprised if it's not.

The Germans don't think this way, however. They simply have to know who they are speaking to at the very beginning of the conversation—even if who they are speaking to is completely irrelevant to that conversation.

I've had versions of this phone encounter many times (in German, of course) and they have never failed to annoy me.

"Hello?" I answered.

"Umm, hello?" There was an awkward reticence on the other side. "Is Sandra available?"

"No, I'm sorry. Sandra is working late tonight. She'll be home around seven o'clock. Can I take a message?" I said, which was amazingly polite considering I was no longer under a blanket.

"Who am I talking to?"

"You called me." I held the phone away from my head and looked at it incredulously, shaking my head. "I can give Sandra a message if you'd like. Or, you can call back after seven."

"But who is this?"

At this point my patience evaporated—not unlike the heat from my blanket—and derision set in. "Do you know everyone that might answer the phone at Sandra's house?"

"No." She sounded defeated.

"Well, then, I don't see how knowing my name will help. So, how about you tell Sandra you left a message with Barack Obama. That's pretty cool, right? A president. Do you have a message for the Commander in Chief?"

"I'll call back later." There might have been some disgust in her voice.

I hopped it wasn't because she was racist. "OK. Have a good night. Don't forget to vote."

So, considering my dislike for how the Germans handled phones, I wasn't terribly understanding when my German daughter asked for one of her own. "Absolutely not," I said. "You don't even know how to answer one." And the conversation ended there.

For a while.

Sandra and I were preparing dinner and chatting about how our classes were going when Emma came in. She sat down next to Sandra and asked if she could help grate cheese.

"I'm almost done," Sandra said, "but you can stir the vegetables on the stove if you want to help."

With a nod, Emma picked herself off the chair and went to the stove. The three of us cut, grated, stirred, and listened to a classic rock radio station.

After a few moments of stirring, Emma broke the silence. "Dad, can you stir these vegetables?"

"Do you want to cut this bread?"

"No."

"Then carry on, my wayward daughter," I said. "There will be peas when you are done," I sang.

Sandra groaned in the background. I glanced over just in time to catch a half smile and an eye roll. When I turned back to Emma, she was crying. She put the wooden spoon down and ran out of the kitchen.

"What was that about?" Sandra asked.

"No idea. I assume it wasn't my singing, though."

"Should we go talk to her?"

"Nah. You know how she is. Let her cry it out for a bit. We can see what's up at dinner. It's almost ready anyway."

A short while later we sat the table and called the kids in. David came in first. "What are we having?"

"Tuna casserole with cheesy garlic bread."

"Can I have something else?"

"This isn't a restaurant, kiddo." I lowered my eyes and nodded towards his chair. He sat down. I poured him a glass of milk and planted a little kiss on top of his blond head, ruffling his hair with my free hand as I turned back to the refrigerator. Emma dragged herself in and took her place, eyes red but no longer leaking.

"Emma, honey, why were you crying earlier?" Sandra asked.

"Because of the kids at school."

My dad-instinct had been piqued. "What did they do?" I asked.

"After class one of the boys went around and got everyone's cell phone number for a class group and I was the only kid who didn't have a phone."

"Really? The only one?" Sandra asked.

"Yeah. Everyone has one. They get to talk about homework and stuff and I can't. It's not fair."

"Why do they have phones already? You kids are too young for phones." Sandra said.

"I don't know, but everyone has one." Emma answered. "I need one, too."

"No," Sandra said. "You don't need one. None of you need one."

Emma poked at her food and didn't answer.

David took advantage of the silence and steered the conversation towards French children's stories. His kindergarten teacher had started a project to teach the kids some basic French vocabulary and since he had learned a handful of those words, he thought he was fluent and was proud of that fact. The phone conversation was forgotten for the time being.

After dinner, Sandra and I split up the kids per our routine: I made sure Emma had brushed her teeth and then read to her from the book we were working on, and Sandra did the same with David.

After shuffling Emma off to bed, and giving David a good-night kiss, I joined Sandra in the living room with the first of my nightly beers in my hand.

"So, what should we do about Emma?" Sandra asked.

"I don't know." I sat down next to her and she threw her legs over mine. "It's a pretty shitty dilemma."

"I don't think so. She's ten years old. She doesn't need a phone." She shrugged her shoulders dismissively.

"I tend to agree, but I can see the appeal. There have been times when I wished she had one — like that time a few months back when I freaked out when she didn't come home from school. I was one phone call away from calling the police, when—"

"That was bad, but still. She's ten." She flung her legs off of mine and came in for an upper-body cuddle. "Besides, a phone wouldn't help your anxiety anyway. You always find excuses to get nervous."

"Point." I took a swig of my beer. "But, if it's like she said and all the kids have one, that changes things."

"No, it doesn't." She looked up at me like I was crazy.

"It does. After kids get phones, that's how they organize their lives. And the kids who aren't part of that world get phased out."

"But phones are horrible for children. The research coming in all points in the same direction."

"I know. I've read it, too, but still—"

"Maybe we should mention how bad phones are at the next parent's meeting. Maybe we could encourage them to take the phones away from their kids."

I looked down at her like she was the crazy one. "Good idea. Parents love it when elite university snobs like us show up and tell them that they are raising their kids wrong."

"Well, they are."

"The truth won't save you, my love." I lowered my head and then brought it back up for a drink.

"Then what are we going to do?"

"I don't know. We need a compromise of some sort. We can't be so clinical about something that makes her cry."

We talked it through for a few more minutes and came up with a plan we could both live with.

After dinner the next day, we called Emma into the living room. She sat in the corner chair, rather than squeezing in between Sandra and I on the sofa as I had expected.

"OK, baby girl," I said, "your mom and I talked about you getting a phone and here's what we've decided. For now, we are not going to get you a phone."

She exhaled and slumped into the chair.

I ignored her and went on. "The research is pretty clear: smart phones are terrible for the mental development of children—they are entirely too distracting. I see it all the time with my students. Some of them can't even pay attention to me for a whole class without checking their phones. Me." I extended my hands to emphasize the point, lighten the mood, but she wasn't impressed. "A phone can ruin your ability to concentrate, so you can't have one."

Her shoulders slumped further and she looked at her feet.

"But," I continued, "we also know that young people today essentially live online and kids who aren't part of that online world, get left out—and that would be bad for your social life. We don't want that, either."

She looked up.

"So," I went on, "here's our idea. You can create an account on my phone and use it to snap-chat or chap-shat or whatever you kids do these day."

"But I can't take your phone to school," she said.

"True. And you're not going to have a phone at school for quite some time. But, instead of watching TV after school, you can have some phone time — or a little of both if you wish. Mix it up: chap a shat and then watch some cartoons."

"I don't know," she said looking back down at her

shoes.

"Think about it," I said. "This is as good as it will get for a while."

The next morning at breakfast Emma came into the kitchen looking more optimistic than the day previous. "Is it true what you said yesterday about your students not being able to concentrate?" she said.

"Yeah. I might have exaggerated a bit, but yeah."

"So, they can't, like, read a book for a while without checking their phone?"

"Some of them can't, no."

"I don't want that. I like reading."

"That's smart of you."

"So, can I give them your number for the homework group?"

"Sure. You don't even have to tell them it's my number if you don't want to."

"OK." She took a bite of her yogurt. "Dad?"

"Daughter?" I raised an eyebrow.

"I don't know how long that will work for."

She was right. Our obstinance to the new culture wouldn't be a realistic parenting strategy for long. We could probably hold out for a few more years, but at a certain point we'd have to give in so that she wouldn't suffer socially. It was a fight we couldn't win.

I sat down at the table and sipped my coffee.

And if it was true for German kids, it was also true for Germans in general. It wasn't fair of me to expect them to accept a hello as a phone greeting. I couldn't change their culture any more than my daughter could change hers. So, if I didn't want to be continually annoyed, I'd have to change how I answered the phone when I was in my pajamas.

I still refuse to answer with my name but, in an effort to mitigate the discomfort on the other end of the line, I now answer with other names. A *nom de téléphone*, my son's teacher might say. Sometimes I'm a president. Sometimes I'm a rock star. And sometimes I'm a character in a book.

Anything is possible when people call the house looking for Sandra.

Lecture Notes on German Nipples

German is hard. For an English speaker, it's nearly impossible to figure out why objects without genitalia get to have a gender and little girls don't. My friends tell me that it's best not to think of grammatical gender as gender at all, but something else entirely. And they would have a point except they are wrong. They are connected. *Der Manager* is a man, while *Die Managerin* is a woman, and humans who aren't comfortable identifying as one or the other have no choice but to pick one, which is pretty ridiculous since there is a third, neutral gender in German marked by a *das*, but I'm told you can't use that one to talk about adults. A little girl, yes, but not an adult.

So, the best way I can wrap my head around it is to imagine the words themselves have a gender and this may or may not agree with the people they refer to. A word with a 'der' attached is not unlike a dinner table with a penis attached—it's clearly masculine even though it will never fix a car.

Unfortunately, this system doesn't work either because sometimes words change their article.

Pizza, for example, is feminine unless I want a piece if it. The pizza tastes good. "Die Pizza—feminine subject — schmeckt fein." Can I have a piece of the pizza. "Kann ich ein Stuck von der Pizza—masculine object—haben?" I would like to think this happens because Germans are progressive, but I know that's not true. So, it's hard. Part of me knows it would be easier to remember if it were the other way around—masculine things become feminine when I want a piece of them—but I hate that part of me.

But I must say, aside from some weird grammar, parts of German are easy. I like the compound words because if I know the parts, I can usually figure about the whole. Since I know 'Kinder' and 'Wagen,' it's pretty easy to figure out 'Kinderwagen'. It's a transporter for children, a stroller. A 'Krankenwagen' transports the sick—an ambulance. A 'Lastwagen' transports loads, so that's a truck—or maybe a testicle. So, all things considered, it's pretty easy to learn German vocabulary.

Sometimes, however, Germans coin ugly words. Horribly ugly words that do no justice to the beautiful things they name. I learn these words, but I hate them and have no intention of using them. I am, of course, thinking about the word 'Brustwarze,' the German word for nipple.

At one point in their past, the Germans looked at one of my favorite things in the world, the nipple, and named it by combining 'breast' with 'wart.' To the Germans, the nipple is a breast wart.

It's nearly unforgivable that the same word for the tumorous growths found on witch's noses is used in the word for nipple. And, more importantly, warts are high on my list of things I never want in my mouth, so that alone should prevent them from being associated with nipples.

How did that even happen? At some point was a man licking a nipple and think, "You know, this is a lot like Aunt Helga's nose, we should call these things breast warts"? I don't know what's worse: that someone thought that way or that the other Germans of the time agreed with him. And all of this ignores the further injustice in calling the areola the Brustwarzenhof, which roughly translates to "the breast wart's courtyard." What is wrong with you, Germany?

But, I'm not here to criticize, I'm here to help. So, here are my suggestions, as an outsider, for alternative words for 'Brustwarze':

Number one. Well, the first one is a bit lewd, but I think it still works. Tittenknubbel. Tit bump. It's simple and direct, but I'm still not sure how I feel about bumps in my mouth — it reminds me of herpes, so it's not perfect. But, on the other hand, I do like saying it. Tittenknubbel. So, let's put a pin in that one for now.

Number two: Brustknopf, the breast button. Buttons have lots of cute associations. Plenty of women love their button noses, for example, some grandmothers collect buttons, so why not have breast buttons? It's true that I don't want to think about a grandmother's breast buttons, but I don't want to think about their nipples, either, so that consideration is moot. But, as a person who likes video games, I rather like pressing buttons, so that association could be worse.

Number three: Milchhahn, the milk rooster. My thinking here is that since the Wasserhahn, a water faucet—but literally a water rooster, spits out water, the nipple could be called a Milchhahn for the same reason. Plus, another word for rooster is 'cock,' so, finally, women could also have a body part named after a rooster. Ultimately, I am in favor of equality— and I like that part of me.

Confession of an American on Halloween

A woman was speaking bad German to her kid on the bus yesterday. If I had to guess, I'd say she should have been speaking Polish, but that assumption is only because she had an attractive, round face, not because I have any knowledge of what a Polish accent sounds like. Since I'm being honest here, I have to say that all Eastern European languages sound the same to me, like various sneezing consonants have been combined with vowels only cats can pronounce naturally. If anyone ever said "Cześć" or the more formal "Dzień dobry" to me, my first instinct would be to say "Gesundheit" or maybe scratch them behind the ear.

It wasn't the first time I had seen a mother denying her child the opportunity to grow up bilingual; sadly it seemed to be a relatively common thing in Germany. From conversations I'd had with foreign students and immigrant friends over the years, the consensus seemed to be that one important facet of the integration project was to leave the old language behind. This never made any sense to me. In fact, I found the notion slightly offensive.

Briefly, I considered explaining to the mother that growing up bilingual was really good for kids, and it was sad she felt pressured to abandon her native language. But, I pushed the thought out of my head almost immediately. For one, it really was none of my business. For two, I recognized I was making unsupported assumptions—maybe she spoke Polish at home and German was just the outside language. But the most important reason was the third: Generally speaking, mothers don't want to get parenting advice from large men in zombie costumes—the dead eyes, mottled skin, and bloody wounds don't exactly inspire confidence in knowledge of early childhood development issues.

The costume, while an odd choice for a bus ride, had been a decent choice for the English department's Halloween party. We thought it would be fun to show up in costume for our Friday classes, even though it was a day early. The department chair had suggested we build a lesson around whatever we had dressed up as, and then meet at the end of the day in one of the larger classrooms for snacks and a few drinks. Jim went as a pirate, Mateo as Benjamin Franklin, and Marcus came as the lead singer of Weezer. Actually, now that I think about it, maybe he had forgotten to wear a costume.

I didn't prepare any lesson around my costume — I couldn't figure out a pedagogical reasons to watch *Night of the Living Dead* or play *Resident Evil* in an English class. So I just pretended I was hungry because there weren't any adequate brains on campus. But, the bit didn't get any laughs, so perhaps it was too intellectual for a zombie costume, or, more likely, my zombie alter-ego had been right.

My German students knew about Halloween of course, but it still wasn't very big. It was getting bigger, but most of the growth was with the younger generation. So, it was a good opportunity to teach them a little something about the only holiday in America that has something for everyone: kids dress up as their favorite characters and get free candy; teenagers and college students dress up as sexy nurses, devils, and librarians and get to go to parties populated by sexy nurses, devils, and librarians; the adults get to put their kids into costumes and take them around the neighborhood; and for one magical night, the elderly get visitors (as long as they have a light on indicating they have candy). Halloween is a perfectly designed holiday.

When I was a college student in the States, my girlfriend of the time and I hosted the annual Halloween party for our friends, which we called the Drunken Pumpkin Fest. The idea, as you might guess, was to drink as much cider as possible, carve pumpkins, and then break the rules of logic by drinking more cider. Years later in Germany, I re-established a version of the Drunken Pumpkin Fest in order to teach my kids and their friends about America's perfectly designed holiday. And no worries, dear reader, I didn't allow them to participate in the drunken part of the party. The cider was for me. Well, me and whichever adult guests were brave enough to drink fermented apple juice with a zombie.

Part of the reason the Polish mother was occupying my mind was that Halloween was on my mind. Halloween was an immigrant holiday. At some point in American history, the broader American society noticed that the Irish immigrants were putting candles in pumpkins and wearing masks and thought, "You know, that looks like fun. I bet it would be even more fun if we added candy," and modern Halloween was born. How could we get new, fun holidays in Germany if the immigrant population felt ashamed to maintain their culture?

The answer was obvious and depressing, so I decided I wanted to know more about why so many of my fellow immigrants were disinclined to spread their language to their children and their culture to the wider German society. I was sure we could improve upon whatever festivals they had by adding candy and fermented fruit concoctions, and it was a shame we wouldn't have the opportunity.

Confessions of an American on Halloween

I took out my phone and sent a message to the only Eastern European I knew, Svetlana, the mother of Yulia, one of my daughter's friends. I explained that the Halloween party that we had invited Yulia to, which was schedule for the next day, was also open for the parents if they'd like to stay and drink cider. Svetlana was a former business student of mine, so I didn't think she'd be too adverse to hanging out with me at the party. Shortly before my stop, she wrote back and said it sounded like fun, so I sent to same message to the other parents on the invite list in the hopes that at least a few would agree to drink with me so Svetlana wouldn't feel weird by staying.

The bus dropped me off a few blocks from my son's day care center. I shuffled my way out and crossed the street. David's day care was situated between two high schools so it wasn't uncommon to see students filing out and heading for buses when I picked him up. When I spotted a group of preteens ahead of me on the sidewalk, I started to drag one leg behind me and moan. When I got close, I reached out as if to grab them. They shrieked and then giggled. I started laughing and continued on my way, without dragging a leg behind me.

David's daycare had had their own Halloween party, and when I got inside, a grin plastered itself on my zombie face as I marveled at the costumes the children were in. Unlike my university students, the younger Germans were well integrated into the

Halloween tradition. But as I made my way through the halls towards David's room, I couldn't help but notice how many of the costumes were of American figures. Superheroes like Spider-Man and the Ninja Turtles were around every corner being stalked by, and stalking, the cowboys and astronauts. A few Japanese characters were present as well, mostly in the form of Pokemon and ninjas, but Europe was poorly represented, which was odd since Germany is in Europe. There was one pirate, a few witches, and one red ridding hood, but that was about it, aside from a few princesses, of course, but I suspected many of those were actually Disney princesses and not European princesses like Descartes pen-pal, Princess of Elizabeth of Bohemia. I didn't blame them: it was hard for kids to get excited about a historic figure who so elegantly criticized the notion that an immaterial object could interact with a material one, and rather easy to get excited about fictional figures who sang to birds while wearing nice dresses.

When I got to David's room, he spotted me through the window and came running, his cape flapping behind him. "Daddy!" He looked up and took a step back. "What's wrong with your eyes?"

"Nothing. I'm wearing zombie contacts." I leaned down, tilted my head, and extended my zombie hands. "You like them?"

He took another step back. "No. Can you take them off?"

"Out." I stood up and smiled. "And yes, I will take them out when we get home. Come on, grab your stuff."

The morning before the kid-friendly Drunken Pumpkin Fest, Sandra and I got the house ready for the guests. We set up and a pumpkin-carving station in the kitchen, an apple-bobbing game on the balcony, and pin-the-entrails on the zombie game in the hallway. Shortly before the guests were set to arrive, the kids went to put on their costumes and I went to put some cider into a glass.

The doorbell rang and I jumped off the sofa, nearly spilling my drink. When I stood up, I shook my head and chastised myself for acting like a teenager awaiting a date. As I made my way into the hallway, I saw that Emma had already opened the door. Because of the Iron Man mask, I didn't recognize the kid, but his size was a good enough clue that it was one of David's guests so I knocked on his door and told him that his friend had arrived.

After a few more guests and still no one to talk to about immigration issues, I started to lose hope. I was about to send a message when the doorbell rang again. And there she was. Svetlana. Emma squealed and dragged Yulia into her room. Like most of the Russian women I had met, Svetlana was thin, attractive, and fashion conscious. I smiled, we shook hands, and I invited her in. "Are you ready for some cider?"

The kitchen was a crowded with pumpkin carvers and parents talking. Germans love to hang out in kitchens, which is something I never really understood. Why hang out in a room with uncomfortable wooden chairs when there was a perfectly good sofa in the living room? I had asked my friends this on a number of occasions and the answer was either, "I don't know. I've never thought if it before," or, "the kitchen is where the heart is," which, while more informative than the other answer, was no less bizarre. "The kitchen is where the stomach is," would have made sense, but what kind of heart doesn't come with comfortable seats?

After filling a glass for Svetlana and topping myself off, I asked her if she wanted to join me in the living room were there was more room and fewer disemboweled pumpkins. She nodded and we relocated. I sat down with a satisfied exhale. "Mmm. The kitchen might be where the heart is, but the living room is where the ass is," I said.

She scrunched up her face. "I don't think I've heard that one before."

"People say it." I lifted my glass and then took a drink.

We chatted about what she had been up to since last we saw each other in class and how Yulia was doing in school. After a while, the conversation turned towards my kids. "Emma came over after school one day last week. She's a great kid. You did something right with her."

"She's great as long as she's not interacting with her brother. When they are together I want to strangle them both."

"I was like that with my little brother, too." She took a drink of her cider. "Where did Emma get that cute costume by the way?"

"I made it."

"Really?"

"Yep, she wanted to be Harley Quinn — that's the Joker's girlfriend in the Batman comics — but I couldn't find a non-sexy version of the costume, so I made one."

"That's so cool. I wish my husband would do stuff like that. He wouldn't think it was manly."

"I think it's pretty manly."

She looked up with narrowed eyes. "How so?"

"Well, I was drinking whiskey most of the time. Plus, who's more manly: the one worrying about what other people think like some insecure teenager or the man drinking and using power tools?"

She giggled. "I hadn't thought of it like that. But, I don't know if a sewing machine counts as a power tool."

"Mine does. It has an incredible Hulk sticker on it."

Emma and Yulia came up to us. "Dad," Emma said, "are we going to go trick or treating later?"

"Yeah. It goes from six to eight."

"Do I have time to carve a pumpkin?"

I looked at my watch. "Yeah, you've got about an hour. Plenty of time. You want any help?"

"Can you draw me a scary face?"

"I can with an example. Why don't you go get me a picture of you from when you were a baby."

"Dad," she said as a two-syllable word.

"OK, fine. Get me your pumpkin and a marker."

Emma perked up and ran off. Yulia, not having understood what we had been talking about, looked a bit surprised by Emma's sudden departure and asked Svetlana, in German, where Emma had ran off to. And after a brief translation, Yulia ran off, too.

I turned back to Svetlana and asked her if she and Yulia were going to stick around for the trick-or-treating. I wanted to ask if Yulia spoke Russian, but I wasn't quite sure how to bring it up.

Now, I'm going to tell you something very strange, dear reader, but I swear it is true: it was she who broached the subject with me. "Do you always speak English with your children?" she asked.

I'm sure my face lit up. "Of course," I said.

"But don't you feel weird when people stare at you in public?"

"No. I don't care what people think about me. I'm a man with power tools remember? Besides, I've never heard any complaints. Usually, people think it's cool that my kids will grow up as native English speakers."

"It's not like for us. When Yulia was little, her

teachers told me to stop speaking Russian to her because she was having some troubles with German."

"Emma had some troubles too, so we sent her to a speech therapist. I don't know if she had a stutter because she was learning two languages at once, but it wouldn't have mattered anyway. Taking English off the table was never an option. And it was never even suggested."

The girls returned and I drew a face for Emma. Satisfied, she directed Yulia to join her in the kitchen to carve it.

"It's different," Svetlana said.

"What's different? The pumpkin?"

"No. Speaking English. English is cool."

"So is Russian." I shook my head in surprise.

"It's not the same. People stared at us. I felt ashamed." Her sentences had slowed down, gotten simpler.

"Ashamed?" I lowered my eyes and shook my head. "You speak the language of Dostyevsky, Tolsty, and Nabokov. Not to mention philosophers like Kropotkin and Bakunin. That's cool. And any German who makes you feel bad about that isn't worth thinking about."

Her eyebrows pulled together in disbelief. "You've read Nabokov?"

"Of course. He's one of my favorite immigrant writers."

"You must like Russia."

"No. I don't. I like Russian writers, philosophers, and artists. But the current government is terrible. If Putin were to ever be assassinated, I would watch it on repeat until I couldn't masturbate any more."

Her eyes widened and she looked down at her drink.

"But, anyway, that's neither here nor there," I went on. "It's good for kids to grow up bilingual. It helps them learn other languages later, opens up more opportunities for books and movies, and, in my case at least, it allows them to talk to their grandparents and cousins."

"Yulia can't talk to my mom without me translating," she said to her drink.

"You should have never let assholes do that to your family," I said. And when the silence fell on the room, it was clear that it was the wrong thing to say, even though I had meant it.

She looked up, her eyes had taken on a glassy sheen. And she left the room.

I took a drink of my cider and closed my eyes. Damn it, I thought, I am an asshole.

When I worked up the courage to leave the living room, I put my glass down and went into the hallway, thinking I should find Svetlana and apologize. I heard the water turn on in the bathroom and waited to see who it was. It was Svetlana; she had washed her face.

"Svetlana, listen, I'm really sorry. I didn't mean to make you upset. I just—"

"I'm not upset with you, Rob," she said, and I flinched. Getting punched is preferable to hearing your name spoken by a sad woman. "I think you're right, but it's too late, you know?"

I wanted to say that I didn't think it was too late at all, but I had said enough for one evening. I pressed my lips together and nodded. "Should we see if the kids are finished with the pumpkin?"

Svetlana and I helped the girls finish the pumpkin and then it was time to get the kids ready for the most important part of the night: the gathering of candy from strangers. I helped some of the kids find missing costume pieces, touched up some makeup issues, and they were ready. The bigger kids headed out on their own, and Sandra went along with the little ones. I said my goodbyes to the final, lingering guests and closed the door.

The house was quiet.

I went out on my balcony with a fresh pint and sat listening to the street. The character of the cacophony was different from the typical street-noises, and after a time, it was clear why. Reader! It was the sound of children trick-or-treating, and nothing but that. The ring of a doorbell, the growl of a werewolf, the squeal of a princess. Halloween had come to Germany. But when my glass was approaching empty, I heard new sounds, sounds of parents calling to their children, ushering them inside. I closed my eyes and finished my drink. The hopelessly poignant thing was not that

I heard German voices, but that Russian was absent from that concord.

Supporting the Boys

I had read on the internet that the most painful part of a vasectomy came in the days that followed — the swelling that needed to be kept down with frozen peas, the dull ache that would barely be mitigated by ibuprofen, and the tension that would build up only to be released by a potentially bloody orgasm. All terrible things to be sure. But for me, the most painful part was feeling the doctor's scalpel slice into something which hadn't been properly numbed.

I didn't scream, but I did tense up and inhale sharply before choking out enough words for the doctor to understand things weren't going well downstairs. In hushed tones entirely too calm for the situation, he said something to the nurse that I didn't quite catch and she left. I could hear her talking to the people in the adjacent room, which I had learned on a previous visit was the laboratory, and was happy to hear the German word for anesthetic, *Narkose.*

As the staff next door shuffled around, I lay there wincing while the doctor held my scrotum together. Between flashes of pain, I couldn't help but think about two of my best friends, Mateo and Stephan. Being adventurously gay, I was sure they had been in the similar situation of a relative stranger holding tightly onto the downstairs boys. And since Stephan was diabetic he might have even had the scrotum-holding experience while another person ran around the house looking for a syringe. But I knew neither one had ever been in this exact situation because vasectomies were straight-men problems.

The nurse came back in and handed the doctor a syringe. "Everything will be better soon," he said to me.

I barely felt the prick of the needle and after a slight warming sensation I didn't feel anything. "That's better," I exhaled.

A short while later, the nurse turned on a machine and the doctor explained it was to cauterize the cuts. I had never heard the word 'kauterisieren' before and was thankful it was a cognate; medical procedures involving genitals are less stressful when you understand what the German doctors are saying. After a few minutes of popping noises that sounded like a bug zapper enjoying the swamp air, the doctor moved to the other side of the table. As he was getting his tools organized, I started to shiver. The light above the operating area was warm, but I couldn't feel much of anything in that area anymore, so it didn't do me any good. Compared to the rest of me, it was a small area after all.

"I might need another shot on this side," I said.

He pinched a section of my scrotum. "Do you feel that?"

"Yes."

He grimaced and grabbed a different finger full. "And that?"

"No, not really. Just pressure."

He nodded. "OK. We'll go in here."

For the first few seconds everything was fine and I started to relax. And then a blinding flash of metallic pain nearly caused me to pass out. Every muscle tensed. The doctor picked up the syringe and started stabbing and injecting. As before, the pain turned to warmth and then feeling was gone. I exhaled. There was nothing to do but wait for it to be over, and be thankful that I didn't have three testicles.

When they had finished up, the doctor asked me to sit up. I did and the room swam under my operating table. I shook my head in an effort to get the room to snap back into focus and anchored my hands at my sides. The doctor put his hand on my shoulder and asked if I was OK. I nodded. He gave me after-care instructions and asked me drop in after the weekend so he could make sure everything was all right. I raised a concerned eyebrow and he quickly assured me that everything would be all right.

While getting dressed, I felt better. If I had been able to wear my wool sweater during the procedure, things would have been considerably more tolerable. And when I slipped into the snug briefs I had brought with me, per the doctor's request, I understood their appeal. My genitals needed the supporting hug of a soft friend.

Once outside, I noticed that Sandra had sent me a message asking how things had gone. I didn't tell her about the problems with the anesthetic, so I shot her a message assuring her that everything had gone fine — she was in Switzerland for a conference for the next few days and I didn't want her to worry.

Since I had my phone out and the downstairs attention had brought them to mind, I sent Mateo and Stephan a message to ask if they wanted to meet up for lunch the next day. By the time I got off the tram, they had written back and I had a lunch date.

***

While depictions of gay men in the media had improved over the years, anyone operating under Hollywood assumptions of what gay men looked like would not have been able to guess the Mateo and Stephan were gay. The image of the thin, fashion-conscious, slightly effeminate, dramatic, best friend of a cosmopolitan-holding New York woman was about the opposite of what I was scanning the restaurant for. I was looking for two relatively tall, bearded men with geeky t-shirts stretched over more-than-ample mid-sections. Lumberjacks at a comic book convention.

It didn't take long to spot them. I waved and headed back to their table. "Sorry I'm late," I said. "I'm moving kind of slow today."

Shortly after I sat down, a man walked by our table. I noticed Stephan's eyes following him and then he scoffed.

"What? Did you just get cruised?" I said.

"Aww, he knows about cruising," Mateo said with a smile.

"Hey," I said, "I'm hip to the gay community."

"We know," they said together.

I looked around for a waitress and when I spotted one, I held up an empty beer glass from the table next to ours and pointed at it. She nodded. "So," I said, "do you guys want to get together this weekend? Maybe play some video games? I'm free on Saturday."

"We can't," Mateo said. "We're going to a bear event."

"What, like at the zoo?" I was a bit surprised by their plans. I knew that they liked cats, but I never took them for the zoo-patron types.

"Ahh, no," Mateo corrected. "A bear is a big, hairy gay man. It's that kind of party."

"That's a pretty specific party. I'm surprised I hadn't heard about that before. I might have to retract my earlier hip-statement."

"It gets more specific than that," Stephan said. "There are polar bears, black bears, cubs—" He counted on his fingers as if the fingers themselves held knowledge of bears.

I raised a suspicious eye. "Wait. Polar bear and black bear make sense, I think, but what's a cub?"

"A young-looking bear," Mateo said.

"OK, good. As long as you guys aren't gluing merkins on fat kids or rubbing them down with minoxidil, I'm cool with it."

They looked slightly shocked, but then laughed — probably after remembering who they were talking to.

"Gross," Mateo said. "No, nothing like that."

"So, if big and hairy is the main thing, then I'd imagine there aren't too many Asian bears."

"Not too many, no," Stephan said with a note of disappointment.

"You should call them pandas," I said. "Those are rare Asian bears."

They both giggled. "That's a good idea," Mateo said. "I'll be sure to mention it at the next board meeting." He folded his arms on top of his middle and looked for the waitress.

"All right, now I'm interested. What if there's a skinny, hairless guy who wants a bear. Can he come to the party?"

"That doesn't really happen too often," Mateo said. "Gay guys who consider themselves bears tend to like other bears."

"OK, but what about a thin, hairy guy?"

Stephan perked up. "Ohh, we have those. They're called otters."

"Seriously? That's too cute. I think I'm jealous."

"Why would you be jealous?" Stephan said.

"I wish straight people were that organized. When I was younger, if I could have gone to a gathering of tall men and the short, big-breasted women who want them, I would have been in heaven."

The waitress dropped off my beer. I nodded a thank-you, and we ordered.

After the waitress left, Mateo turned to me and smiled. "Nobody in the gay community is going to feel bad for your dating troubles, you know," he said.

"Well, they should. We've got problems, too. It's hard out there." I took a drink of my beer.

"No. For you, it's really not," Mateo said, suddenly serious.

"I guess. Being tall is kind of awesome."

But he was right, of course. Sure, I didn't have access to the kind of organization that my gay friends had access to, but straight people didn't really need that level of organization because there was essentially no risk in asking a woman out. Gay men took on risks that I never had to worry about, so it was no surprise they had developed systems to allay the perils of gay dating: code names, secret handshakes, colored bandannas—a secret society open to any man with the need for more penis in his life.

Straight guys don't need the protection of secrecy. We can operate under the assumption that everyone is straight and statistics pretty much guarantee we won't run into problems too often. In all my years of dating, I had only asked out one lesbian.

"Oh, I'm sorry, but I'm not really interested in penises," she had said.

"Really? Well, OK. I guess I can tuck it. I can make a pretty nice man-gina."

She had to stop herself from spitting out her beer, and the effort caused her breasts to heave just enough to remind me why I had approached her to begin with. "Well," she said, "I would like to see that, but no. What I mean is—"

"I know what you mean. I was just joking around. You wanna throw a game of darts anyway? I'm sure my friends will be in the bathroom for a while."

Mateo repositioned himself when the waitress came around with the food. The chair was too small for him. He folded his arms over his belly as well as he could and waited for the waitress to finish putting the plates down.

"Do you have plans for next weekend?" Mateo asked after the waitress had left.

"I don't think so. You guys wanna hang?"

"Yes, but the Christopher Street Day parade is on Sunday and we wanted to ask you to come to that."

"Shit, that's right. I forgot about that. Yeah, I was

planning on going anyway. Take the kids. Make a family day out of it." Even though I had spent a good amount of my teenage years in gay clubs—not because I was gay, but because I was a young punk kid with pink hair and the gay community was the only one in my small Michigan town that didn't try to kick pink-haired kids' asses—I hadn't heard of Christopher Street Day until I moved to Germany. After I learned about it, I became an instant fan. It combined a few of my favorite things: loud music, sexual people, and, most importantly, celebrating an event in which normal people made cops fear for their lives. It was beautiful. And, it even had lots of leather outfits, so it gave me ideas for Sandra's Christmas presents.

Stephan giggled. "How are your kids ever going to rebel against you and Sandra?"

"I don't know. I guess they'll become evangelical Christians."

They both shuddered.

"How are they doing by the way?" Mateo asked.

"Ruining the world."

Mateo knitted his eyebrows together. "Your kids?"

I smirked. "The kids are doing fine. Emma started fifth grade and is doing very well—last week she got to teach her English class when her teacher had to meet with the principal. And David is doing well despite having minor socializing problems, but his teachers are all impressed with how smart he is."

"That's not a surprise," Stephan said. "If you and

Sandra had dumb kids, I'd have to abandon my acceptance of evolution."

"Aww, thanks." I lifted my beer in toast.

"It would be good if you came to the parade," Mateo said. "We've heard rumors that some right-wing types want to stage a counter event."

"Assholes," I said.

"Seriously." Mateo nodded in agreement. "Anyway, we've been trying to remind everyone to come out. Show their support."

"We'll be there. And I'm always down to bash the fash if things go in that direction."

"It's not going to be like that," Mateo said. "They probably won't show up at all, but thanks for offer."

The waitress came back to check on us. Before she left, I ordered another beer and handed her my empty glass.

We ate in relative silence and after finishing, I told them I had to pick up the kids from school. Two hugs later, I was at the bar to pay my tab.

***

Sandra came home from her trip about an hour after I had put the Emma and David to bed. I was cuddled up in my bath robe working my way through a bottle of wine and Ralf König's Kondom des Grauens, a terribly funny comic about a detective trying to catch a monster that looks like a condom and eats penises. There was a bag of frozen peas under my robe working double-duty: keeping both my glass and the sore cellar pleasantly chilled.

"You look comfortable," Sandra said. She plopped her backpack on the empty chair in the corner and then draped her jacket over it. She was wearing the teal sweatshirt we had bought on out last trip to the States. An uninitiated observer would assume that she had changed into something more comfortable for the train ride, but I knew the truth: philosophers didn't care about clothes and nobody at the conference had even noticed her sweatshirt or that her socks didn't match.

"Thank you," I said. "I'm trying. How was your trip?"

"It was OK." She sat down next to me. "Did the doctor say you could drink?"

"He didn't say I couldn't."

"Did you ask him?"

"Of course not. He said no lifting heavy stuff for a while and no bike-riding for two weeks, but he didn't say anything about no drinking."

"Well, if you're sure." She put her head on my shoulder. "So, how are the boys feeling?"

"Not too bad. A bit sore, but the drugs help. The wine helps more."

"How long before we can resume activities?"

"He didn't say." I took a sip of my wine. "Maybe not tonight, though. It's a bit sore."

"I wasn't suggesting. Just curious."

"Maybe tomorrow. Give the lite beer semen a test run."

"Lite beer?"

I held up my glass and smiled like I was an actor making a toast in a commercial. "Same great taste. Less filling." I took another sip.

"Wow. Those drugs are helping."

I smiled.

"It's a little sad, though." She came in for a hug. "Knowing we won't have another baby."

"For me it's a relief. Last time we had a scare, I was terrified."

"We could handle it."

"Yeah, I'm sure we could," I lied. The truth was I wasn't sure I could handle it at all. The last pregnancy scare had lead to a panic attack that lasted for days. It was, more than anything else, the deciding factor behind the vasectomy appointment. I wasn't exactly sure why thoughts of having another baby worried me. I liked babies — at least as much as anyone could like something that couldn't play video games or talk about comics. The fact that people tolerate babies at all is a testament to how damn cute they are. But, cute babies or not, I had always been troubled by the idea I would die early. After turning forty, I became worried that I would be condemning any further children to losing their father at a young age. I knew that these thoughts were irrational, but recognizing that didn't make them go away. If it did, people wouldn't need more than a day of therapy and logicians could be mental heath professionals. But that wasn't the world we lived in. We lived in a world where some people spent years in therapy, some spent years in bottles, and others opted for invasive surgeries.

I was feeling better already.

Talking to Sandra, but not telling her everything that was going on, brought to mind my first panic attack. It happened when I was around twenty. I woke up in the middle of the night with chest pains, my left arm had gone numb, my breath was short, and I was filled with a sense of dread. A heart attack, I thought. I was about to die. My right hand started to shake and I wanted to punch something. My legs started to twitch and I wanted to run.

The doctors later explained to me that this was a fight or flight response and was typical of a panic attack. But I didn't know that then, so I woke up the girl that was in my bed and we went to the emergency room. After a few tests, a doctor came in and explained: my heart was fine, my problems were mental. He told me this probably wouldn't be my last episode, and when it happened again, I shouldn't let myself get too worked up.

He was right. It wasn't my only attack, but it was hard not to freak out. There was always that little voice in the back of my mind: this isn't a panic attack, this is the real thing.

And maybe one day it will be the real thing, I won't go to the doctor, and that will be the day I die.

***

The morning of the parade was the first morning I didn't wake up with a dull ache between my thighs. Skeptical, I stretched out on my back and sent an exploratory hand to investigate. But even with some prodding, everything felt pretty good, so after a shower I slipped into boxer shorts for the first time since the operation.

Once breakfast, coffee, and Saturday morning cartoons were out of the way, we all headed downtown. Neither Sandra nor I were sure where the parade started, but it was clear enough from the decorations that it would end near the fountain at the center of St. Johanner Markt, so we wandered around there looking to see if we knew anyone.

"Are we supposed to meet Stephan and Mateo somewhere?" Sandra asked.

"No, I didn't make any plans. They might be on one of the floats. See if you can spot a bear float."

"There will be bears here?" Emma asked. Her little eyes lit up. "Like at the zoo?"

"No, baby doll," I said. "Not those kinds of bears."

After a bit more walking, it became clear I had made a tactical error when it came to my underwear choice. The downstairs wasn't ready for the freedom of movement that the boxers allowed. I groaned, and

Sandra noticed.

"Are you all right?" Sandra asked. "Should we sit down?"

"No, I'll be OK. The boxers were a bad choice is all. Too much swaying and jostling down there. The bells weren't ready for a *glockenspiel*, and they're playing an angry tune."

"Daddy, what are you talking about?" Emma asked. She pushed her hair behind her ears and looked around. "I don't hear any bells. Just the music from the parade."

"Nothing, honey, it's OK. I'm just having some problems with all the walking."

"We could go home if walking's a problem," she said.

"I'll be fine." I spotted two shaved heads on the other side of the market. "Everyone's got problems, but sometimes other people have more important ones." I adjusted my pants and grimaced. "The boys could use some support."

Going Home

The trip to the States was Sandra's idea. Our trips to America were always her idea. It wasn't that I didn't like my family—I was actually quite fond of them, and it wasn't that I didn't like America—I was quite fond of that, too. But, somehow it never occurred to me to go back. I knew it was there and my family was still alive, and that was enough for me.

It wasn't enough for Sandra; she wanted the kids to have a relationship with the American side of the family. At least that was her argument, and I believed it. But I believed something else, too: She wanted to see Lake Michigan and have an excuse to read vacation books rather than philosophy books. I didn't blame her on either account.

After we booked the tickets, I started to get excited myself. I wasn't terribly interested in seeing Lake Michigan, as beautiful as it is, I had grown up on its beaches, so it didn't look terribly interesting, it just looked like home. What I did want to do was drink enough American beer to drown a bear, play cards with my mom, shop in a places where the staff knew what customer service was, eat as many bagels as I could in fourteen days, and, maybe, see a bear—but that last part wasn't important, or even likely.

I was ready to go home.

When we boarded the train to Frankfurt, the kids started clamoring for snacks—*Reiseproviant* they called it, and I shot Sandra a nasty look. Over the years, she had conditioned the kids to expect snacks as soon as we got on a train or bus that traveled outside the city. It didn't matter that we had just had breakfast, or that we had also just eaten croissants on the platform, or that there was no way more than a few crumbs could fit into their full bellies. The kids were on a train and wanted something to eat and it was Sandra's Pavlovian doing.

I put on my headphones on so I didn't have to listen to their chewing. In addition to bad eyesight, Sandra had passed her resonant skull onto the kids, much to my discomfort. Sure, I probably missed out on a fascinating conversation about dinosaurs, but the sound of people putting food into their heads made me want to put a bullet in mine.

The train from Saarbrücken to the airport in Frankfurt stops directly under the international terminal, so it could not be more convenient. After arriving, a short walk and an escalator ride put us just a few steps from where we needed to check in. The check-in clerk informed us that despite booking a Lufthansa flight, we would be traveling with another carrier in their alliance, and while I was a little disappointed I wouldn't be having Lufthansa's better food, it was a minor inconvenience all things considered. Even better airline food is still a microwave dinner.

We made our way through security and after a short wait, boarded the plane. Shortly after take-off, the stewardess came by and dumped a tray of water in my lap. She apologized, but the apology wasn't profuse, so I hated her. A short while later she returned with a towel and a Christmas stocking.

I took the towel and started mopping up the puddle I was balancing on my crotch — I didn't want the water to soak into the seat I had to sit in for nine hours. I figured wet pants and underwear would dry sooner than a seat. When I handle the towel back, she tried to hand me the stocking.

"Here, this is for you," she said. "It's from first class. Again, I am sorry."

"I don't want that."

A look of horror tinged with disgust crossed her face. "But this is from first class."

"Does it have dry underwear in it?"

"No. It has—"

"Then I don't want it."

She walked off and I turned to Sandra to see if she needed any help getting the kids set up with entertainment for the flight. Both Emma and David already had headphones on and were watching cartoons. We normally limited the kids' TV time to about an hour a day, which wasn't nearly enough for them as far as they were concerned, but that rule didn't apply to flights and they were more than happy to watch TV for the entire flight. Once in the airplane, they were perfect travel companions.

"You were mean to that woman," Sandra said.

"She dumped water all over me. I'm allowed to be testy—I have wet testes."

Sandra lowered her eyes. "She was trying to be nice."

"What? With that first class stocking? Did you see how weird she got when I refused it? She acted like I had called her kid ugly or something."

"You should have taken it. I'm sure Emma would have liked opening it."

"Yeah, I suppose. I just didn't like how she expected me to be impressed with something from first class."

Sandra shrugged and opened her book. I dug my headphones out of my bag and hit the button for the stewardess. I needed some music. And a drink.

A flight attendant came by, thankfully not the clumsy one. "Can I help you with something?"

"Yeah," I said. "I'd like a whiskey and a beer,

please."

"Drinks cost five dollars. Euros are fine, too."

"What? I've never paid for drinks on a Lufthansa flight before."

"This isn't a Lufthansa flight."

"My ticket says Lufthansa."

"I'm sorry, sir. Would you still like to order drinks?"

"No." I put my headphones on and closed my eyes, regretting allowing Sandra to convince me to leave my hip flask at home.

When dinner came by later, I caved and bought the drinks. Then it was just a matter of watching a movie, listening to a Ramones album, and watching another movie before the flight was two-thirds over. I walked around the cabin a bit to assure myself my legs still worked after being folded up in what space was afforded to those in economy, and then returned to my seat to read.

I must have dozed off because the next thing I remember is Sandra telling me we were about to land. Once on the ground, we packed up our things, roused some moody children, and made our way out of the airplane. After leaving the confines of coach, it's always a special sort of torture to walk through business and first class and see how comfortable they had it.

After making our way through passport control and collecting our bags, we were out in Chicago

O'Hare's main terminal. I spotted my father and waved. I couldn't help but notice that he had put on some weight back on. By American standards he was still on the thin side of normal, but I knew he fluctuated between thin and rotund and was wondering if he was on the way back to round or if I had missed that period and he was making his way back to thin.

"Welcome home, guys," he said with a broad smile.

"It's good to see you, Dad," I said while putting the bags down and then gave him a hug. "So, are you trying to get back to your childhood physique?"

"Getting there." He smiled.

"Mountain Dew diet?"

"Nope. Exercise. I jog now."

"That doesn't sound like you."

"People change." He gave Sandra a hug and said hi to the kids, who managed smiles and hellos despite being nearly too exhausted to stand. "Come on," he said to the kids, "Let's get to the car so you can get back to sleep."

They nodded weakly.

After getting away from the airport and into Chicago, we had a little trouble finding our way to the highway. Nearly too late, Dad noticed the road we needed, and after making a quick check over his right shoulder, he merged into the right lane and made the turn. Red and blue lights flashed behind us.

"Well, shoot," he said. In our old, poor days, getting

pulled over would have been very bad news. We rarely had up to date insurance or tags, but Dad, like me, had managed to escape poverty in the years since I had moved out, so I was sure he didn't have anything to worry about in that regard.

An officer approached his window, which my father had already rolled down. "Evening, sir," the officer said. "Do you know why I puled you over?"

"Yes, I nearly missed my turn back there. I checked my blind spot, but I don't think I signaled."

"That's right. Do you have a license and registration on you, sir?"

I heard a tap at my window and looked over. Another officer had approached my side. I rolled the window down.

"How are you doing tonight, sir?" he said without politeness.

"Just fine, thank you," I replied.

"Where are you guys heading tonight?"

I shook my head, a bit surprised by the question. "That's not really any of your business."

"No reason to get rude, sir. I'm just making conversation."

"I wasn't trying to be rude."

"You have ID on you, sir?"

"Yes," I said, but made no motion to get it.

"Can I see your ID, sir?"

"No."

He bent down and looked in the car. "Sir, I asked

to see your ID."

"I heard you, but I'm not going to show it to you."

"But I'm asking to see it."

"You're within your rights to ask. And I'm within my rights to say no. You didn't stop me, you stopped the driver, and your partner over there already said it was for merging without signaling, so there's no way this counts as a Terry stop for me. So, I don't have to show my ID." Not only had my work for the police in Germany more or less erased my fear of police, it had also taught me a few things about the law.

"A Terry stop? Are you a lawyer, sir?"

"I don't feel like continuing this conversation," I said, trying not to sound rude.

"Sir, I don't like the way you are talking to me right now."

"Then stop talking to me right now," I said, this time trying to sound rude.

I heard the radio of the officer dealing with Dad squawk and then then he handed the documents back and told us to drive safe. He then told the partner at my window they needed to go. As we pulled away, Dad shot me a nasty look. "What was that all about? Why didn't you just show him you ID?"

"Because he had no reason to ask me for it."

"It wouldn't have been a big deal."

"I think cops overstepping their authority is a big deal. Don't you remember the 80s. You used to joke about how the Russians were treated. 'Show me your papers,' and all that."

"You're lucky they got called away. They probably would've given me a ticket because you were impolite."

"It's not like I was recording the encounter to put online or something."

"Things could have gone bad. That's all I'm saying."

I shrugged. "Maybe."

We eventually found our way to the highway and despite my better efforts, I fell asleep. When we pulled into a gas station, the bright lights woke me up. "Where are we?" I asked.

"Just outside of Benton Harbor," Dad answered.

I nodded and looked in the back seat. Sandra and the kids were sleeping in various uncomfortable positions. I turned back around. "I was out for a while. I'm glad I slept through Indiana. Dirty fuckers."

"Hey, come on. Watch the language."

"Sorry, Dad."

Most Michiganders hated Indiana and I was no different. There were lots of good reasons for the ire, but the most important was that they did their best to pollute Lake Michigan. Of about sixteen hundred miles of Lake Michigan shoreline, only about forty miles were located in Indiana and rather than protecting the natural beauty of the only beautiful thing in the entire state, they invited some of the dirtiest companies in America to dump pollution into the lake. As a kid, my dream was for Michigan to start a war with Indiana to take over their part of Lake Michigan so that it could be better protected.

Dad hopped out of the car and started pumping the gas. I joined him. It felt good to stretch my legs.

Back out on the highway, I fell asleep almost immediately. When we got to Dad's house, I carried David inside. Rachael, my dad's second wife, was still awake and told me she had made up beds for us in the basement. I nodded and carried David down, took off his shoes and covered him up.

I went back upstairs to say hi to Rachael properly. She hadn't changed at all in years. Still the same shoulder-length black hair, the same blue-green eyes, the same freckled cheeks. If our lives had gone in a different direction, she would have been a striking beauty. Since Dad had had me at an irresponsibly young age and she was younger than him by at least a decade, that put her only slightly older than me.

But now she was a step-mom, so I didn't look at her that way at all. She was family. She looked like Michigan.

***

The following morning, jet lag being what it is, Sandra, the kids and I all woke up well before the Michiganders. Not wanting to be rude house guests, we hung out in the basement, reading and playing with toys until we heard movement upstairs.

Dad was making coffee and Rachel was sitting at

the kitchen table reading the paper when we all filed up from the basement. I asked the kids what they wanted for breakfast and got to work exploring the cabinets. After getting the kids situated with some candy masquerading as breakfast cereal, I got to work on my own breakfast. The refrigerator was filled with many of the foods I fantasized about in Germany, so coming to a decision wasn't easy. But, ultimately, I couldn't resist a chipped ham bagel sandwich with pepper jack cheese and spicy mustard.

When I started to spread the mustard Dad quipped, "You need to put that away. It's too early to smell horseradish."

"Sorry, man. The clock might say seven, but my body says it's two in the afternoon. A perfect time for a ham and cheese bagel with lots of spicy mustard." I put the rest of my sandwich together and made a cup of coffee. "Hey, do you guys have any salt and vinegar chips?"

"I wouldn't tell you even if we did." He chuckled and pulled a carton of eggs out of the refrigerator.

I went over to the table and sat down between David and Rachel.

"Daddy, I'm not any more hungry."

"You're not hungry *any more*," I said. "But, yeah, OK. Put your dishes over there in the kitchen."

He hopped down from his chair and did as I had asked.

"He didn't finish his cereal," Rachel said.

I shrugged. "That's OK. We don't want the kids to stop eating when their plates are empty. We want them to stop eating when they are full. It's silly to gauge hunger by whether or not there's still food on the plate."

She nodded and smiled. "That makes a lot of sense, actually."

"Yeah, it's kind of weird how in the old days parents tried to train kids the other way around."

"Is that something you learned over there?"

"No, I don't think so. I don't know how we got the idea. German parents are a lot like American parents with the clean-your-plate thing. We probably read it somewhere and it made sense."

Sometime after lunch, I heard the door open and knew it had to be family because there had been no knock. I put my book down and went to the kitchen. Mom was taking off her patch-work coat, which looked to be one of her home-made creations. I made a metal note to ask her how to make coats. Seeing her reminded me it was time to learn more sewing machine tricks. And hearing her come in without knocking made me wonder if I would be comfortable with Sandra coming in my house without knocking if we ever separated. I doubted it. Maybe because we hadn't meet, reproduced, and split up all before high school graduation. Or, maybe because maintaining relationships with exes is crazy.

"Hi, mom."

"Oh, it's so good to see you, honey." We hugged. "Where's Sandra and them babies?"

"They're not babies anymore, Mom, but they're around here somewhere." I called for the kids and took a seat at the kitchen table. Mom pulled off her sweater and put it on the back of the chair. Her waist-length blonde hair had grown thinner but hadn't grayed.

The kids came running up the stairs and nearly knocked mom out of her chair with their greetings, and then, both speaking at once, they tried to tell mom about everything of interest that had happened since she had last seen us: new cat, new school, video game bosses—a jumbled cacophony of things interesting to children.

The kids eventually ran off and mom and I could exchange our own stories. Hers were variations of the same depressing events that had defined most her life: trouble finding full-time work, unsafe working conditions when she did, exploitative temporary job agencies. Many of the students I'd had at Brandt could tell similar stories, but the difference with them was they could tell them to me, their teacher in a private school who was being paid by the State to help them find jobs. I could do almost nothing to help my mother, and the State wasn't interested in helping, either.

Dad came in from the garage and my mom turned around. "Bob, can I use your car? I need to get some smokes and mine's acting funny."

"Sure. The keys are hanging by the door. I can take a look at your car this weekend."

"Thank you, honey." She got up from the table and pulled on her sweater. "Does anybody need anything from downtown?" she said to the house.

"I'll go with you," I said. "I want to get some beer."

"Well, come on, honey. Where do you need to go for beer?"

I knew finding good beer in America wouldn't be a problem; microbrews and craft beers had been well established for quite some time. But I wasn't interested in those. It wasn't that I had anything against pumpkin spice ales or cookies and cream stouts, or whatever other hipster thing was trending at the moment, but I was craving a normal, mass-produced American beer. The kind of beer that was really only tolerable when it was ice cold and served in a can. There was no need to go to a supermarket or dedicated liquor store staffed by people with man-buns and beards. "Gas station is fine."

When we got out on the road, my mom turned on the radio. After the commercial break, the host of the show launched into some ill-informed diatribe about why he wanted charges of sedition brought against members of the press.

"What are we listening to?" I asked.

"Oh, I don't know," Mom said, a touch of sadness in her voice. "Talk radio, I guess. Your dad likes listening to these guys."

"This stuff is crazy. Can we change the station?"

"Sure, honey, let's find some tunes."

I shuffled through a bit until I heard a few bars from The Who.

"Ooh, I like this one," my mom said.

"Me, too."

The closest gas station was ten minutes away. I had forgotten how much driving was involved in my hometown. Closest grocery store—fifteen minutes, movie theater—twenty minutes, shopping mall—twenty-five minutes. And all of those times were on highways or fast country roads. Only the mailboxes were within walking distance.

Once inside I was struck by how big the gas station was. I had been there many times before, but had somehow forgotten. To the left of the doors was a sandwich shop with at least five tables for the guests. Directly in front of the doors was the main shopping area. They didn't have much except candy, chips, and various dipping sauces, but they had rows and rows of those things. I didn't want any junk food, but I looked around anyway just to see what they had and to check on their prices. The convenience stores in Germany are unbearably expensive, which is mostly because the gas stations can stay open after the grocery stores have to close, and the prices reflect their monopoly status.

After perusing more flavors of chips than I had

seen in years, including a few I had never heard of before—Parmesan shrimp pasta stuck out as particularly disgusting—I headed back to the coolers.

All of the classic beers of my teenage years were on display. I grabbed a case of Budweiser cans—not Bud Light of course but the full-fat variety. Growing up, Dad had called them Bud Heavies, so in addition to the fuller taste they came with nostalgia. I put the case on the counter and said hi to the portly lady behind the cash register—partly to be nice and partly to tell her she needed to stop talking on the phone about tonight's party at Ray's house and do her job.

"ID?" she said.

"Excuse me?" I wasn't sure I had heard her correctly. I hadn't been asked to show my ID at a gas station in years — Germans rarely ID teenagers for beer, let alone middle-aged men.

"I need to see your ID for the beer."

"I'm not pretending to be a middle-aged man, I really am one." I smiled.

She did not return my smile. "Everyone has to show ID. It's store policy."

"Oh. That's, ah, well, that's stupid, but whatever." I dug out my passport and handed it over.

"What's this?"

"A US passport?" I tried not to sound too arrogant. I knew Whitehall wasn't the most cosmopolitan city in the world, but finding a gas station attendant who didn't know what a passport was was still shocking.

"I've never seen one of these before." She opened it and put it on the counter. "I'm not sure we can take them."

"Of course you can take them. It's a US passport." My diplomacy dike was groaning.

"Does it got your birthday in it?"

"Yeah, it's right here next to the picture." I tapped its location.

"Well, OK. I guess you're old enough. That'll be $12.96."

***

Two weeks later and a few days before our flight back to Germany, Dad had a party. Shortly after dinner, the guests started to arrive. I knew some from the neighborhood, but there were also a few unfamiliar faces. After I read the kids a goodnight story, I went out to the garage to get a beer. Dad was there talking to my mom's on-again, off-again boyfriend of the past ten years, Mark.

"Hey, Rob," Mark said. "Try this." He handed me a mason jar filled with clear liquid.

"What is it?" I held the jar up to my nose and sniffed.

"It's good. An old friend brought it up from Kentucky." There was a mischievous grin tucked under his grizzly-Adams beard.

I took a tentative sip and regretted it. "Bleh. What is it?"

"Moonshine." He chuckled.

"It tastes like hell."

"It'll put hair on your chest."

"It better. Then I might forgive it for burning the hair off my tongue." I shook my head, took a deep breath, and took another sip. "How do you know it's not wood alcohol?"

"Those Kentucky guys know what they're doing."

"Good enough for me," I said. "Let's get some beer chasers and play some cards."

It didn't take long to find some Euchre partners. The game was more popular in Ohio, which was where Mark was from and had learned to play it, but was popular enough in Michigan to get a game going if we happened to be at a big enough gathering. Sandra agreed to be my partner and an egg-shaped woman I hadn't met before agreed to play with Mark. After we sat down, she introduced herself as Janice, a friend of Rachel's.

The first few hands had Mark and Janice up by a few points, but then Sandra managed to win a loner hand—a hand so good she didn't need my help to win—which put us in the lead. Mark and I alternated sips and head shakes from the mason jar.

Christina, Mark's teenage daughter from a previous relationship, came up to the table. She was a nice kid and had babysat for us a few times over the past few weeks so Sandra and I could see a bit of Whitehall's nightlife. "Hey, Sandra, what do you think of this shirt I got today?" she said, doing a little runway turn to show off the shirt, a tight babydoll t-shirt cut high enough to show off just a touch of midriff.

"Aww, that's super cute," Sandra said. "It looks great on you."

"I would love to wear something like that," Janice said, "but I couldn't. It's not fair that fat girls get looked down on for wearing sexy clothes."

"But that's the thing," I said, "they're not sexy when fat girls wear them. Clothes are supposed to make you more appealing. Skinny chicks are already appealing so they can show a little skin and make things even better. You can't do that."

Sandra's eyes widened and she shook her head, but I continued, "Buy yourself a muumuu. If you can hide that muffin top long enough, somebody might throw a shot into you."

Mark coughed and nearly spit out the moonshine he has just sipped.

"I like you," Janice said. "You don't mince words."

"That I don't." I took the jar from Mark and sipped.

"So, do you have any other advice for a fat girl?"

The moonshine was starting to cloud my judgment, so I couldn't tell if she was angry and hiding it well or really wanted to continue the conversation. "Play to your strengths," I said. "That's all I'm saying. I'm not trying to be mean. You seem nice. I'm just saying there are guys out there for just about every body type, you just have to find them. Two of my best friends are big guys. Real big guys. They love they way they look and they love each other. I know there are straight guys out there like that—you know, guys who like big girls." I emptied my beer. "Maybe get a t-shirt made: Will Suck Dick for Relationship. It even almost rhymes."

"I don't do that."

"Wear t-shirts with rhymes?"

"No. I don't, umm—"

"Oh, you don't do *that*. Well, in that case, go buy yourself some cats and embrace single life." I tried for another sip, but the beer was empty. I got up to get another.

The garage was getting cold so I wasted no more time out there than I needed to. When I stepped back in the kitchen, I heard the pitter-patter of little feet coming up the stairs. David poked his head out from around the corner. "Daddy, where's mommy?"

"You need to go back to bed, kiddo."

He looked into the dining area and saw Sandra sitting at the table. "Momma, ich kann nicht schlafen," he said.

I heard Janice mock his high-pitched, and, to her, unintelligible sentence. David looked down, cheeks reddening. I took a step toward the table. "Don't tease my boy for speaking a different language." I took another step, the room swam, I turned around a puked in the sink.

I ran some water to wash out my mess and then went downstairs. I still had enough stamina to brush my teeth and then I collapsed on the bed.

When I awoke the following morning the bed was empty. I wasn't sure if it had ever been filled by anyone but me. I went to the bathroom to splash some water on my face and then upstairs to pour the biggest cup of coffee I could find.

Sandra was sitting at the table reading a book with a dragon on the cover. Dad was making breakfast. "How you feel this morning?" he said with a raised eye.

"I've been worse. I'll be fine after a pot of coffee." I got a cup out of the cabinet, filled it, and then went to sit beside Sandra at the table.

Dad continued to cut green peppers. "So what do you think about all of the refugees coming into Europe?" he asked.

"I don't think much about it," I said and then took a drink. "It's a big project to be sure, but Germany's rich. We can afford to take care of people who need help."

"I heard on the radio that there has been an increase in crime."

I shrugged. "That's not surprising. Of course crime will go up if you add a million people to the population. Especially if those people are in desperate situations."

He grimaced and continued to cut.

"Actually," I continued, "the only thing that angers me about the situation is that the States isn't doing more to help. The richest country in the world with space to spare and they take in almost no refugees. It's pathetic."

"No, it's good," he said. "I don't want those people here. I don't want them living next to my family."

Despite what appeared to be not-so-subtle racism, I thought I'd give him a chance to explain. "What are you talking about? What do you mean 'those people.' They're just people. People trying to escape a horrible situation. They could come here and open some restaurants or whatever. It would be cool. I don't think I've ever had Syrian food."

"No way. We need to keep them out."

"But that's what's cool about America," Sandra interjected. "So many different cultures in one place."

"It's too dangerous," Dad replied.

"No, it's not," I said. "Sure, there are certain risks, but they can be mitigated. And sometimes it's worth a little risk to do a lot of good."

"*They're* not worth it."

My eyes widened and I balled my hand into a fist under the table. "What the fuck is wrong with you? They're just people." I could no longer hide my disgust, but I lowed my voice. "Besides, the US bears some responsibility for what's happening over there."

"They attacked us first," he said, shrugging one

shoulder dismissively.

"What? No they didn't. Syria has never attacked the US."

"That's what you say."

"Yeah, I like to say true things."

"You say it's true."

"Listen, I don't care about your political opinions—thcy are irrelevant to me—but you can't disagree with the facts. Facts don't work that way. You can accept them, or you can be wrong. And right now, you are fucking wrong."

He pointed in my direction. "I'm your father and I don't want to hear that kind of language in my house."

"The only offensive language in this house is yours," I snapped. After taking a breath, it occurred to me that I wasn't sure what he meant by the comment. My first thought was that it was because I had sworn. I knew that he and the rest of my family didn't much care for that, so that was an obvious reason for his comment, but I wasn't sure. If the little ones had been around, I would have accepted that as an explanation, but none of them were, and besides, they were my little ones anyway.

He sat down at the other end of the table and took a bite of his breakfast burrito. I went outside.

Alan Ginsburg once wrote that he had seen the best minds of his generation destroyed by madness. As I fumed in Dad's garage, the words struck me as apposite. Ginsburg was talking about great minds ruined by drugs and I was thinking about average minds ruined by this new tribalism in the US, but the parallels were there and I did want to howl.

But after cooling down, I realized I was wrong. His comments were nothing I hadn't heard from him before. The only difference was I had forgotten he thought that way, and I wasn't able to tolerate it anymore.

In the days that followed, I said nearly nothing to him. I didn't go out of my way to be reticent, but merely buried myself in the work I had brought with me from home. It was easy to avoid conversation with a red pen in my hand, an English essay in front of me, and my headphones on.

The night before our flight, we all went to a seafood restaurant. I had mentioned to mom that Sandra had never had Alaskan King Crab, so she, unbeknownst to me, reserved a table for all of us at one of the local places that served it. Sandra and I offered to pay for everyone as a thank you for feeding and housing us.

We all settled into our chairs and the server came around. "Can I get you started with some drinks?"

"Sure," I said. "What beers do you have on tap?"

"I'm sorry. We don't serve beer."

"Oh, OK. Then I'll have a red wine. Nothing too expensive. A California Cabernet would be fine."

"I'm sorry, but we don't serve alcohol of any kind."

As soon as she said that, I remembered that the

liquor license laws in Michigan were, in a word, stupid. The number of licenses was limited, so when a new restaurant opened, they would have to wait for a license to become available. If they didn't want to wait, they could buy a license from a business that already had one—a pub that was going out of business for example, but this was normally too expensive for most restaurants to bother with. Things could have been worse, however. In some places in the States, it's not possible to buy alcohol at all—they're called dry counties and, strangely, they exist in the places most in need of escape, places like Tennessee. In fact, Jack Daniel's whiskey is made in a dry county which means they can't sell their product at the distillery. But they do sell collector's bottles which just happen to have whiskey in them. A laughable loophole that the police ignore, and that gave me an idea.

"I understand," I said to the waitress. "I'm sure the cooks in the back have a green bottle with cooking sherry in it. How about you sell me an unopened green bottle? That way you are not serving alcohol, but just selling me a bottle, and I can enjoy dinner with my family?"

"I can't do that. I could lose my job."

"It was worth a shot." I looked back down at the menu. "I'll have a cranberry juice."

After dinner, the kids asked if they could watch a movie with at my mom's. Sandra and I happily agreed on the grounds that packing would be a lot easier without kids running around.

Folding a shirt, Sandra asked, "Are you going to try to patch things up with your dad?"

I didn't look up from my own folding and packing. "No."

"He's family."

"I don't care about that. Shared DNA or not, he's a racist."

"So, what? We're not going to come here again? After one fight? That's not fair to the kids. They love it here and it's important for them to have a relationship with their American family." She folded up a shirt and placed it in the suitcase.

"There ain't nothing that smells worse than a black man."

She looked up, noticeably shocked. "What?"

I looked backdown at my own pile of laundry. "He said that to me when I was twelve. I had become interested in the civil rights movement." I shook my head and grimaced. "I don't remember what prompted it. Maybe a teacher, maybe I wanted to know more about what Public Enemy was rapping about.

"Anyway, I made my way through Alex Haley's biography of Malcolm X, then *Roots*, Dr. King's speeches, stuff like that. I eventually found my way to Baldwin. I don't know how many times I've read *Nobody Knows My Name*, but that's the book that first planted the seed that a poor kid like me could move to Europe.

"At some point I said something to Dad—maybe he had made an off-color remark, I don't remember—and that's what he said to me." I picked up a handful of dirty socks, stuffed them into my suitcase, and then looked up at Sandra. "This wasn't our first fight. This was our last."

The following morning, Dad drove us to Chicago. We took his Blazer so we would have enough room for Mom to drive down with us. The trip was quite.

At the drop-off location in front of the terminal, we all piled out of the car. I went to the back to take out the luggage, which I piled on the curb. The kids gave my mom hugs and said their goodbyes. When she looked up from a hug from David, I could see that her eyes had gone misty. "It was so good having you all here," she said with a slight tremble.

"It was nice to be home," I replied and gave her a hug. "We'll see you again soon. Maybe you could come and visit us for Christmas."

"Oh, I would love that."

With a nod, I thanked Dad for the ride and picked up the two suitcases. When I stepped through the doors into the terminal, a thin smile spread across my face as I looked for the check-in counter.

I was ready to go home.

About the Author

Robert McGee the author of this book, like Rob McGee the character in this book, is an American who moved to Germany to be with a German woman, teach English, and make German babies. It turns out he's pretty good at all of those things. His writing has appeared in *The American Bystander*, *Little Old Lady Comedy*, *Points in Case*, and a number of other places in print and online. This is his first collection of true stories that never happened. You can follow him on Twitter @Robert_McGee